The M
Of
War

a fantasy novel by

Damon Alan

This book is dedicated to my critique group, you know who you are, and to my wife, without whom none of this would be possible.

Contents

Chapter 1 - The Chinese Dragon

July 11, 1940

Terrified, Lieutenant Heisuke Abe raced over the treetops, his Ki-51 at war emergency power. The plane screamed, the engine roared, and the bullet holes in his left wing whistled as he tried to maintain control.

His tail gunner, Lieutenant Aketo Nakamura, worked hard to keep the panic from his voice as he yelled commands at Heisuke, all of which the pilot ignored.

"Today we die, Heisuke, today we die!"

"Has it happened yet?" Heisuke barked. He jinked the aircraft to the right and downward into a ravine. A river flowed at the bottom, at various points as rapids and other times in deep slow flows. "We might make it if we can get hidden and stay that way."

"Did you see what happened to the American? We're not going to survive this."

"The P-40 that shot holes in our wing?" Heisuke asked. "He's dead and we're not. I'm flying, not sightseeing."

"Look up."

"*Chikushō*!" Heisuke yelled over the roar of the fighter's engine. Several hundred meters up the P-40 was in a flat spin, smoke trailing in a spiral above the plane, with a large section of tail missing. As Heisuke watched, the pilot leapt from the plane, narrowly missed by the damaged tail as it spun around.

"The thing ripped the tail off," Aketo added. "I saw it."

"Where is it now?"

"I can't see out of this ravine."

Heisuke glanced upward again, over his shoulder. His heart pounded in his chest, he forced himself to focus on saving his life and Aketo's. The beast looked to be fifty meters long and even wider side to side with wings outstretched. Surprising him once again with its speed, the creature shot over the ravine a kilometer ahead where the river gorge widened.

The Ki-51 tilted back and forth as he fought to keep it off the ravine walls and stay below the upper level of the gorge. Death was an instant away it seemed, the only question was if it would be by crashing or by being an appetizer.

"The creature swung back around and grabbed the American pilot out of the air," Aketo informed him twenty seconds later. Horror tainted Aketo's next comment. "Now it's eating him!"

"You saw that?" Heisuke asked.

"As it disappeared over the lip of the gorge."

"We're ditching the plane," he told Aketo. "That monster is

looking for us, and if it finds us we're dead too."

"Are you crazy?"

"It's our only chance. It's faster than we are, and the gorge narrows again before it opens up once more ahead of us. Once we clear the narrow walls, it will attack us there."

He didn't wait for an answer. The river deepened and slowed down just ahead of him, in a location where the gorge was no more than twenty meters across. He pulled back on the throttle, the engine noise died away.

"Today we die, Heisuke, today we die!" Aketo cried out.

Heisuke understood his friend's fear, even as he was embarrassed by it. When he'd first seen the creature, he'd soiled his own flight suit.

It was a dragon.

Had the Chinese summoned it? A creature of their mythology to fight for them? If so the dragon wasn't very well controlled in its actions. First it took out the American plane as the P-40 and Ki-51 fought over the ravines northwest of Ya'an. The town, burning below as Heisuke and Aketo raced southward trying to survive, was burning.

Somewhere in the area more Americans fought. Whether they fought the dragon or Heisuke's squadron mates he had no idea.

Or maybe they were all dead. The dragon was much faster than any of the planes, including the one he was about to ditch.

The aircraft shuddered as it approached stall speed, then

dipped downward. Heisuke pulled back on the stick just before hitting the river, causing the tail of the plane to strike the water first. Aketo yelped from the back. The rapid deceleration caused by the drag of the river water slammed the front of the plane down. The nose cowl caught after the propeller blades ripped off.

The aircraft rolled up on its nose, then slowly fell over, facing the opposite way, top down into the water.

Behind him Aketo shrieked.

"Unbuckle," Heisuke screamed, then his head was covered with water. At the same time he yelled, he followed his own advice.

He slipped his arms out of the harness and pushed downward into the river, leaving the cockpit. The flow of water was clear, tinted green, and cold. He slipped back up into the cockpit to grab a small bag he always flew with. It contained a few pebbles from the Shinto shrine near his home.

Looking aft, he noticed the gun seat was empty, so either Aketo was dead and drifting downstream or he was out and heading toward safety.

The plane was sinking, but for the moment one wing was in the water and the other canted upward toward the lip of the gorge. This gave Heisuke something to hide under, catch his breath, and survey the surroundings.

Holding onto the lip of the cockpit, he rose to the surface and broke the water with just his head. Twenty meters downstream, swimming at a slight angle toward the shore, Aketo furiously breast stroked, slapping the water loudly.

"Toward the shore, to the right!" Heisuke yelled.

Willows lined a narrow bank, densely packed and fully fleshed out in leaves that would hide them from the sky.

Had the fool swam straight toward the shore, he'd already be there.

The plane groaned and started tilting forward. The heavy engine was going to drag it down.

Heisuke sucked in deep breaths then dove underneath the aircraft hoping to make it to the edge of the river unnoticed. He swam ten meters to the shoreline, the scrape of rocks against his fingers the first sign he was going to make it. He raised his head momentarily to get a breath and look for the willows. He'd gotten turned around and missed them by several meters.

The plane, behind him now, was downstream a bit with only a few meters of the tail sticking out of the water. A hundred meters away Aketo stood on the bank, taking off his flight jacket and surveying the surroundings.

A shadow blotted out the sun, and a deep air-sucking roar sounded like a childhood memory from his Uncle Isamu's forge filled the canyon. The dragon, wings skimming just above the canyon walls and stretching out wider than the gorge itself, raced down river. Its head, on a long neck, hung downward into the ravine. The roaring sound stopped as the creature spat fire past Heisuke's position.

Aketo died in a furious conflagration.

The creature rose back toward the sky and disappeared over the lip of the ravine. Heisuke sank below the water before pulling himself the few meters upstream to the willows. Entwining himself within them, he kept his body submerged although the water was growing brutally cold. The pebbles he'd saved from the plane hopefully had a bit of protection left in them.

Nothing but his face exposed above the surface, he breathed shallowly and awaited his fate. The willows obscured the sky, providing a small comfort to him. At least he wouldn't see death coming.

Chapter 2 - The Call Home

Resting in a stand of trees, Irsu Crackstone looked over his amassed forces. Five hundred of his dwarven troops, and another thousand human troops assigned to him by the Swiss General Henri Guisan. It would appear his meeting with Guisan's attaché, Eugen Hager went well enough that Guisan trusted him to lead some of his men.

The commander of the human troops, Captain Conrad Hurst, rarely left Irsu's side.

The relationship he'd developed with Hurst was a strange one. Being in such close quarters with the human helped Irsu learn the ways of these strange people a little better. Clearly the information handed out by Hagirr before the Day of Joining wasn't accurate. The humans were capable, intelligent, and committed to most of the same values Irsu held. The captain was even making a very honest effort to learn Dwarven and was doing quite well with it.

The reality didn't fit the mythology of humanity at all, even that which didn't come from Hagirr. On Aerth, after ten thousand years of absence, the humans were thought of as barely more than animals. Beings who responded more to urges than thought.

Maybe ten thousand years ago this was true. But most of the Swiss Irsu had met so far seemed exceptional in both intelligence and resourcefulness.

It took Irsu some time to get over his biases and realize victory for the Lost Hold depended on trusting the Swiss. He also made great effort to learn the language that Hurst spoke, which he called German. Irsu had soldiers learning it as well, including Numo. Coragg, Irsu's second in command, complained about any such requirement, but was trying.

"Their language makes me spit all over myself," Coragg complained when Irsu told him to stick with it. "A wet beard is a smelly beard."

"Trees. German line," Captain Hurst said, interrupting Irsu's thoughts in his slowly improving Dwarven. He gestured toward a line of forest over ten *dokadros* away. "And you smell already, Coragg."

Coragg sputtered as the three soldiers looked over the rise they hid behind. Their small copse of trees was bordered on the north by a berm, probably containing the rocks pulled from the fields between them and the next stand of trees.

The Germans, known to Irsu a few months ago as The Grays, were the same people the dwarves fought so hard to get through moving toward Nollen. These soldiers, while intimidating to the other humans, were nothing special.

Still, it didn't pay to underestimate an enemy.

"Do they have catapults?" Irsu asked Hurst.

A puzzled look was the response.

Irsu picked up a rock and simulated the noises he'd heard when the Swiss had bombarded his unit. "Thump," he said as he swung his arm upward to simulate a catapult's lever. The rock sailed in an arc, and when it hit the ground Irsu said, "Boom."

Hurst laughed. "Cat-apult? *Nein*. Is called artillery."

Artillery was the human word for whatever they used in

place of catapults. Obviously better than catapults, if Irsu was being honest. He pointed toward the trees. “Artillery?”

“Yah. Some.”

Irsu turned to one of his platoon commanders who’d moved closer to learn their situation. “Get your men under cover. Dig holes. Set this as our line for today. We advance at night, so tell those who can to get some sleep. Nobody leaves this area. If the Germans see us and use their artillery, we die. Tell the other leaders.”

As the platoon commander moved off, Coragg rested his hand on Irsu’s shoulder. “Digging in is good, Iron Commander, but I have been working on a tactic for the open fields.”

“What sort of tactic?”

“Sort of an arrow shield, but in all directions.” Coragg waved at a group of soldiers standing in the trees. “My testers have taken to calling it the beetle.”

Irsu was intrigued. “Let’s see it.”

Coragg snapped his fingers and pointed at the soldiers. Clearly, he’d intended for Irsu to see this. Fifteen seconds later the dwarves were under a dome of shields. Around the base were a few holes, but the rifles the Swiss had given them quickly projected from them. Twenty dwarves, in short order, looked like a dome fort complete with defensive armaments.

“And you think that will be effective?” Irsu asked. “Can they move?”

Hurst sneered. “This is way to die. Artillery does not care about your shield!”

“I was about to say that I don’t think it’s going to be effective against bombardment from enemy,” he paused to mouth the next word carefully, “ar-til-lery, but that is something I don’t think we can save ourselves from. And the dome can move,” Coragg replied, looking annoyed at Hurst. “I think this will be effective against the fast spitter sticks.”

“Machine guns,” Hurst corrected.

“Move west along the tree line,” Coragg ordered the men.

The dome moved at a tenth the walking speed of a dwarf, which was already slower than most races.

“The enemy will just pick up their guns and move to a different location,” Irsu said. “What will this accomplish?”

“Retreat?” Coragg said. “Some defense is better than none.”

“You do have a point there,” Irsu agreed. “But a crawling child could follow you at that speed.”

“We’ll keep working on it.”

Irsu looked over the small rise again. Numo said the Germans were in the trees ahead of him. Hurst said the same. But he didn’t see anything.

A flash of light caught his eye, up in one of the trees so far away. He stared at the location for a second.

Something hit him in the side of the face with the ferocity of a rock beetle’s bite. He spun sideways down the incline, landing on his back at the feet of Coragg and Hurst.

“Sniper!” Hurst yelled and started waving everyone down

toward the ground.

Coragg leaned over Irsu.

Irsu looked up at his friend, feeling confused as to what just happened. His ears rang and a stinging sensation was starting to burn on his cheek.

"Flesh wound. Not going to kill the likes of you," Coragg said as a Swiss medic knelt down next to him. "But you're going to be even uglier now."

The medic slapped what looked like white cotton on the side of Irsu's face, and the cloth stuck to what felt like wetness.

"I'm bleeding, aren't I?" Irsu asked. Numbness stretched across his face and seemed to permeate his head. Events unfolding around him seemed surreal.

"Just a scratch," Coragg replied.

Hurst slunk over like he was hiding from an Elven archer. "There is a sniper in the trees," he said in German. "You were very lucky, Commander Irsu."

"What's a sniper?"

"Kills from far away, using a rifle… a gun," Hurst answered. "You've got a nice gouge on your cheek there."

"And a battle scar to tell your kids about," Coragg added.

Hurst turned back to the matter at hand, and good for him. Someone had to. "The Germans know we're here. There are probably machine guns waiting for us to cross this field. We'll be slaughtered." He paused to think a minute. "We are going to need a different plan…"

A commotion to the side caught Irsu's attention as a dwarven soldier ran up from the south. The soldier was in full plate, but also carried a tabard that indicated he was functioning as a royal courier. Another dwarf directed the man toward the group of commanders.

Irsu groaned. Royal couriers bearing messages was rarely, if ever, a good sign.

"Get down," Hurst barked at the new arrival as he waved his hands downward.

Everyone understood that gesture. Despite the full plate, the courier dropped to a kneeling position then unrolled a scroll as they invariably did. Even if their message was one sentence it apparently became more official if read when delivered. "Iron Commander Irsu Crackstone, you are summoned back to the court of King Scorriss Bloodstone to resolve a situation by order of the Underking. Scout Numo is to accompany you."

"What situation?" Irsu asked.

The dwarf turned the scroll over and checked the other side, then looked at Irsu blankly. "It does not say."

"It's something outside the hold," Coragg said. "Otherwise you wouldn't need Numo."

"Makes sense," Irsu replied, wincing as a lance of pain shot through his face. "Veznik can look at my face as well. I'll see if Kordina can still love me now that my beauty is marred."

"You're not getting rid of her that easy." Coragg looked at Hurst. "What's the plan with that… as you say… sniper."

“We’ll have to put a few of our own out to see if we can track him down. We’ll need someone to draw fire so we can see his position,” Hurst answered.

“I’ll get a volunteer. Someone with a better helm than our leader,” Coragg said to the human. “Then I’ll be readying Irsu’s things and mine for leaving.”

“You’re going with him?” Hurst asked.

“I’m his second. He’s the *Amblu-gane*. I’d be derelict not to go with him.”

The Swiss Captain did a sweep of the dwarves nearby. “Then who will you leave in charge?”

Irsu stood up, low so as to not get hit by the sniper again. His head was starting to pound, and a few shots of alcohol were in his near future.

“You,” Irsu told Hurst. “This is an alliance. You’re third in command. Now you’re in charge. The King had to know that would be the result when he summoned me back.”

“Then we will be changing our location, as the Germans know it and I fear artillery. I’m honored by your trust, Iron Commander,” Hurst replied. “Even as it’s unexpected.”

“Unexpected?” Coragg scoffed. “You haven’t seen a thing from Irsu Cragstone yet.”

“Shut it,” Irsu replied. “Don’t you have packing to do?”

Chapter 3 – Visitor

Harry's new allies, the Dek, were packing. Horses and strange small camels were being loaded. Nothing was mentioned the night before, no ceremony marked moving day, nobody had said a word to Harry's Squad.

He knocked on the door to Tim and Teeran's *yoglik*, as they had their own now. A nicer one than the British infantry squad shared.

"Come in," Tim's voice called from within.

Harry opened the rickety wooden door and bent over to step inside. Tim reclined on a stack of leather bags, the Dek version of a chair.

"Tea, Harry?" Tim asked, waving toward a copper pot on the central hearth. "You're just in time."

"Yes, please," Harry answered, sitting down on a log bench facing Tim. "You and Teeran seem to be doing well."

"I've never been happier. I feel like I settled into my purpose."

Harry nodded. He understood the sentiment; he missed his own wife more than he'd ever thought possible. "Say, Tim, do you have any idea why all the packing?" Harry waved at the door.

As he did the door popped open, Teeran slipped inside before closing it behind her.

"You might ask her," Tim said to Harry.

So, he did.

"We're nomads, Harry. The Dek I mean. These are the summer grounds. It's getting late. If we want to make the winter grounds, we leave today."

"Why aren't you and Tim packing then?" Harry asked.

Teeran looked at him and smiled, seemingly amused. "What do you mean? What you see here is what we have. It will take no time at all."

"Where are you going?"

"The winter grounds. In the Aldikki Mountains," Teeran replied as she dropped a few leather bags on the bed. She tossed one to Tim.

"Pack," she told him.

Tim lifted himself from his comfortable spot, looking around. "I'll leave out the cups and the pot for now, I'll let it cool after Harry's visit is over," he told his bride.

"Pack," she said again. "Those can be last."

Typical married life banter, Harry thought. He might have had the same with his own wife were he at home. As Tim stuffed their few possessions into bags alongside his wife, Harry asked questions.

"Are we going with you?"

Teeran pointed at Tim. "He is, whether you do or not is up to Grandmother."

It was something Harry would need to think about. Going to a winter shelter wouldn't get them back to Earth. But why in the mountains?

"Why are you wintering where it's colder?" Harry asked Teeran.

"Protection. We leave today to make sure we can get into our shelter. Once the snows fall heavily it will be cut off from the outside."

"That makes sense. What about food?"

"Why do you think there are so many animals with packs? Even the dogs carry their own food to the shelter. Those that can't… well, they become food for others."

The Dek had deer, pigs, horses, the little camels, dogs, and even a few cats. Chickens and ducks as well. Is that all they eat? It didn't seem like enough food for a community. But obviously the Dek knew what they were doing. They did this yearly.

"What about you and Tim? You just got married. Where is your food?"

"My father is expected to provide for this year. By tradition we are supposed to start a family, but that won't happen since he's human and I'm dek. But next year we'll have all summer to hunt together and this winter we'll make things to trade for animals of our own."

Seems like she had it all worked out.

"I'm going to go speak to Grandmother," Harry said. "Thank you both for the tea."

"She's at your *yoglik* waiting for you," Teeran said as Harry opened the door. "Don't keep her waiting too long."

She could have mentioned that sooner.

"I won't."

Harry walked down the winding pathway between the homes of the Dek. People ran all over, animals clogged the walking spaces, and children shrieked as they tried to deal with the excitement of the day.

Finally, he reached the point he'd started, the front door of his squad's *yoglik*.

Inside, Grandmother sat on a log bench, speaking to the rapt soldiers sitting around in a semicircle. The old dek had charisma, for certain. She squeezed the charm necklace that allowed her to understand them and them to understand her. Unlike the medallion Harry's squad had, Grandmother's worked for the speaker and the listener. Something she'd neglected to tell him until he figured it out.

"—and so Hagirr, having secured his own future—" Grandmother stopped her story when she noticed Harry. "I've been looking for you."

"And I for you," Harry replied. "Why didn't anyone tell us about today?"

"The exodus?" Grandmother laughed. "It's such a part of our lives we didn't even think about it. When the shadows of the sun tell us it's time to go, we just go."

"What about us?"

"You have no food stored, Harry," Grandmother told him, looking sad. "Who will feed you when the snow is deep?"

"I will," a voice said through the still open doorway.

Everyone turned to look at the source, except Grandmother, who closed her eyes and sighed.

The scariest looking dek Harry had seen yet stood outside, bent over, looking into the *yoglik*. A female, she was lean and stringy. Her skin was darker than any he'd seen yet, maybe that was a play on shadows… which come to think of it, the area around the newcomer seemed darker even though she still stood in the sunlight.

Private Miller, a few feet from Harry, whimpered. Harry pretended not to notice.

The newcomer looked at Miller and smiled, teeth filed to a point filled the exposed mouth. "Aaaah, you're just who I am looking for."

"Me?" Miller squeaked.

The female entered without asking permission. She wore puffy fur pants, but other than that was nude. Tattoos traced lines across her body, forming intricate woven patterns with scarification. That was the cause of her skin tone. At first Harry thought there must be some trick for his eyes in the patterns, but he soon realized there was no trick. Dim lights pulsed along the lines, almost too dim to be certain they were real. One of the lines moving horizontally along her torso changed its location on her skin, connecting to a different line higher on her ribs so the light could follow a different path toward her neck.

"Ye'r th' scariest wifie a've ever seen," Lars blurted out.

She looked at Lars for a second, seeming to decide he was of no significance, then without a word moved back to focusing on Miller.

"Stand up!" she barked at her new focus.

Miller, to Harry's surprise, did precisely that. Either out of fear or simple subservience, Harry had no idea. But it wouldn't do.

"Now listen here," Harry started.

"I'll get to you," the female promised. "I understand you're their leader. I am not challenging you." She had Miller's lips stretched back and was examining his teeth, something the private was strangely cooperating with. "Plenty of filing opportunity…" she mumbled.

Something brave inside of Harry rose to the surface, and in a fit of either suicidal thought or courage, he pushed his will. "No, you'll get to me now. As you said, I am the leader."

The dek jerked her head toward him, and Harry swore that for a moment her eyes flashed a baleful red. The look of irritation on her features was gone an instant later, replaced by her pointed-tooth grin once more.

"You're bold," she cooed. "I like that. It will be needed in the coming days."

Were she human, Harry would guess her to be about twenty-five. Like a human, she understood sexuality. Even covered in tattoos there was something less animalistic about her than when Harry'd met Teeran, but still definitely sexual and dangerous.

She moved until she was toe to toe with him, then looked up

into his eyes. A mere few inches different, her head tilted hardly at all. Harry could smell her breath; it was a bit like fermented fruit. Her hair was black as coal and twisted into elegant patterned braids that seemed part of her network of lines.

"Are you mated, leader of humans?" she asked.

"I am," he answered. "I am married to a woman who is not on this world."

"Too bad. I like you. Do you humans mate outside of marriage?"

Harry gulped. She was getting to him a bit. "Some do, but I would prefer not to be unfaithful to my wife."

"Wife… do you hope to see her again?"

"I do."

She passed a finger under Harry's chin, lightly dragging a pointed nail just hard enough to catch the stubble on his face. "Then you will listen to me, ogre slayer."

"Ogre slayer?" Miller said from behind her.

The female raised her finger and tapped Harry in the middle of the forehead. "You remember this fellow?"

The room vanished for a few seconds, and the image of a bullet ridden corpse filled Harry's mind. The creature that they'd been forced to kill when they'd first entered this world.

"I do," Harry answered, hoping it wasn't a friend of hers. "That's the giant we killed after he tried to abduct us. When we first arrived."

"While traveling I came across the body," she said, her finger now tracing along Harry's neck. "I asked him who killed him and took the image of you from his mind. All of you."

Harry smirked. "You asked a dead thing who killed it?"

"Surely not the first magic you've seen since arriving here?" she asked him in a throaty whisper, her finger still playing in his stubble.

"No," he conceded. He had no idea why her assertions had even surprised him.

"I trailed the lines you left in the sand. Your transportation leaves quite a path to follow."

Harry nodded. It wasn't like they were going to abandon their lorry and walk when they didn't have to do so. Which reminded him they were at the point they had to. When his squad left the summer village, most of them would be walking. A few had horses now, having traded or earned them in some fashion.

"I found your machine not far from here. It smells terrible."

"The fuel, I expect," Miller said.

She smiled, her eyes never breaking focus on Harry's. "See how he already seeks to please me?"

"What do you mean?" Harry asked. "What have you done to him?"

"Nothing. He senses who I am."

Grandmother huffed. "All this posturing is annoying me."

"Then leave, mother, and I will finish my business with these humans."

"You're Grandmother's daughter?" Harry asked.

The look on the dek's face told him that was a stupid question. She had just called the older female mother. He got no verbal answer.

"Very well," the old dek said, rising. "When you're done with the performance, daughter, stop by my *yoglik*. We'll be leaving in a few hours; it would be good to say a few things before you're gone again."

The new dek shook her head subtly and smirked so that only Harry could see. "I will, mother."

Grandmother ducked out and started singing as she wandered away. The song faded with distance.

"I am Cylethe. I smelled the one I'm interested in at a location not far past where you crossed the Dwarven bridge."

She must be talking about Miller. "Smelled him?"

"It's a bit more than that," she answered, "but that is a term you'll understand well enough."

"Do you need a bath, Miller?" Harry quipped past her.

The men laughed; the tension finally broke a little.

"I am a natural mage, as he is," Cylethe said, ignoring Harry's humor. "I will be training him. And keeping him from attracting the attention of Hagirr."

"Hagirr?"

"Yes," she replied. "The world wizard Hagirr is your way home, Harry, but you'll have to find a way to make him want to send you there. If he were to find you now, he'd either kill you outright or capture you to be taken to the pens."

"The pens?"

"Where Hagirr is holding most humans who come through the gate," she replied, looking angered by the concept.

Harry thought about what Parker had translated from the giant they'd killed. "Was that where the ogre planned to take us?"

"Almost certainly."

He had to get that information back to England. "The ogre failed, and now we're here. You can't send us home?"

She laughed. Then when Harry just looked at her, she shook her head. "Oh, you're serious? No, Harry, I can't open a gate between worlds. Only one mage I know of possesses magic at that level."

Harry sighed. "Hagirr."

She nodded her head. "You learn fast. Good. We will have to travel to the winter lands separate from the rest of my people. I don't want him," she pointed at Miller, "to attract Hagirr's attention and get my family hurt while I'm training him. Once we're underground, we'll be safe until it's time to travel again."

"Underground?" Harry asked.

"You will see in time," Cylethe answered. She finally

lowered her hand, then glanced at Miller.

Harry looked at his radioman as well. "What will you train him to do?"

"Harness his natural ability, of course. He's already taken his first baby steps, we're lucky Hagirr hasn't noticed. Maybe he was distracted by something else. Regardless," she answered, pointing at Miller, "it's time for him to stand tall. It's your only hope to get home."

"Why would you help me?" Miller asked.

She finally turned her face away from Harry's, looking directly at Miller.

"Because when they go home," Cylethe waved her hand at the other soldiers, "you, Miller, will be staying here with me."

Chapter 4 - von Krosigk

July 14, 1940

Ernst Hoffmann sat in an uncomfortable wooden chair across the hall from Elianna, a witch whose power he neither understood nor knew the limitations of. She sat in an identical chair, facing him, her back against the opposite wall.

They were waiting to meet the Führer. Herr Lutz Schwerin von Krosigk. A person who, in Ernst's estimation, was an even bigger idiot than Adolph Hitler had been. With the conquest of Austria, Czech lands, parts of Poland and Alsace-Lorraine in northeast France, Germany had secured control of lands lost in WWI plus more. With the opening of the gate over Rotterdam the Allies had sought a truce. Peace had been restored, with Germany on top, holding the lands it had so quickly seized.

The Fatherland had almost doubled in size and resources.

Then this fool goes and messes that up to start a war with Switzerland. The Swiss, of all people. Fighting them would be like trying to kill a badger in its den. It might be done, but not without wounds to show for it.

"You have worry on your face," Elianna observed.

"This is the leader of my country," Ernst replied. "Absolute leader. There is no excuse for failing him."

"You have failed him?"

Ernst smiled weakly and shook his head. "Not yet, I suppose. I delivered what I promised to Germany. But depending on how you behave in this meeting that delivery may or may not be considered a failure."

"Blunt," she replied. "I like that. But what is it you fear? That I will turn them all into ash? I have no such intentions."

The guards in front of the Führer's office shifted uncomfortably. Each of them probably had a very personal stake in the safety of von Krosigk, such as the well-being of his family.

"Your reputation is known," Ernst whispered harshly. "Speak the wrong words and this meeting won't happen. Speak enough of them or words with enough severity and we'll be led from this building and shot."

Elianna's mouth hung slightly open for a moment. She was stunningly beautiful, in an underfed waif sort of way.

"Do you really think that's something that could happen?" she finally replied, amused.

Ernst sighed. "No, probably not. You could probably easily escape and save me as well if that was your wish. But then you'd have no alliance with Germany, I'd be on the run if I was even alive at all, and there would never be a second chance for you to make your offer."

She pursed her lips. "I see your point." She snapped her head sideways to look at the guards. "I am learning your culture, do not be alarmed. I have Director Hoffmann here to keep me under control. Control I readily submit too."

Again, the guards shifted uncomfortably. The four of them were likely uncertain if they could take her or not. What had Himmler told everyone about the elf?

"Silence would be a better choice," Ernst advised her.

"What's the fun in that?"

The door to the Führer's office opened and Himmler, the devil himself, stepped out into the hallway. "Herr von Krosigk will see you both now."

Ernst stood and turned toward the door, realizing these might well be his last moments alive. That sensation had happened so often in the last months that it no longer really made him feel anything other than a sense that things might finally be over. "Come," he indicated to Elianna with a gesture toward the now open door.

The guards stepped out of reach; Ernst noticed the trigger fingers resting on the triggers of the MP40s the men carried. More than a hundred rounds ready to riddle him and Elianna with holes should the need arise.

"Let me talk at first if you would," Ernst said. "Once we're past protocol the conversation will open up and you can say your piece."

"Very well," Elianna agreed.

They walked past a reception room and into a room decorated with dark woods. Herr von Krosigk sat behind a large desk. Four more guards stood at attention in the corners behind him to the left and right. Himmler walked to a leather couch and sat down next to a woman Ernst didn't recognize. She smiled warmly at Himmler, Ernst, and Elianna, then seemed to brighten up even more when she noticed Elianna's frame and ears. She was so bold to even subconsciously, probably, touch her own ears to feel the comparison.

Ernst snapped to attention in front of the Führer's desk and saluted, waiting to be acknowledged.

"While he's standing like a toy soldier, I'll introduce myself," Elianna said.

Ernst closed his eyes and clenched his teeth. Did she not listen to anything anyone recommended?

"I'm Elianna, consort of Hagirr, Master of Jangik and Aerth," she continued. "You must be the Führer fellow I've heard so much about."

Von Krosigk, looking stunned for a moment, rose from his chair. His mouth hung open and he stared at Elianna, completely ignoring Ernst.

Then he started laughing.

"You are marvelous!" he exclaimed. "You are clearly not human, and," he turned to Himmler, "Heinrich, if I had not seen it with my own eyes, I'd have thought you a man of exaggeration."

"You find me to be a spectacle?" Elianna asked, her tone one that Ernst didn't like at all.

Should he say something?

"Drop your arm, Director, I'm certain you have given the appropriate honors by now," the woman on the couch said.

What the hell. Ernst dropped his arm.

Herr von Krosigk came around the desk and approached Elianna, who seemed undeterred by the massive man. "So, you are… what did you say, Heinrich, an *elf*?"

"I am," Elianna said. "A Desert Elf from the Endless Wastes. A place unlike your verdant and green country."

"Well spoken!" von Krosigk said as if he was listening to a chimpanzee speak. He reached out to touch her skin, the area he reached for erupted into tiny waves of flame. The Führer drew back from the heat.

"I can also do magic," Elianna said almost seductively. "Something you can't do, can you..."

The guards shifted their weapons upward at the first sign of fire, but Himmler waved them down. Von Krosigk looked around, for the first time uncertain as to what he had on his hands.

"You, my precious dear, should call me Lutz," he informed her, his head tilted to see Himmler and Elianna.

"Come sit down, Director," the woman on the couch said. "You're in the way of the show."

Ernst, knowing that he'd lost control, sighed. He walked toward the couch where the woman patted a spot next to her.

"Madam," he said. "You seem to have me at a disadvantage..."

"Ehrengard Freiin von Plettenberg, or von Krosigk if you will," she said, extending her hand.

The Führer's wife. Fantastic.

"The honor is mine, Madam von Krosigk," Ernst said as he kissed her hand then sat beside her.

In the interim the Führer and Elianna continued their peculiar exchange. He seemed to think her a curiosity he could poke and prod, when in fact she was a nightmare, a powerful magician that could summon creatures, burn with fire, or simply rip the soul from one's body.

Ernst was letting his Führer play with something far worse than fire.

"I should like to see you nude," von Krosigk said to the sorceress. "Are you like a woman?"

"And I should not like to see you naked," she replied. "What is wrong with you?"

Considering the Führer's manners, that seemed like a perfectly valid question. But Ernst knew what would come with an unsatisfactory answer.

"Herr von Krosigk, if I may…" Ernst said louder than he should.

The Führer turned to face him, giving him a moment of attention.

"If you will, sir, I've seen Elianna in action. She's not a circus act to be prodded. She's the most dangerous creature I've ever had the displeasure to meet."

"As I told you," Himmler added. "She is dangerous, and you, my Führer, are poking a dangerous bomb."

Ernst looked at Himmler and they shared a moment of understanding. He'd warned them not to act like this. Obviously neither von Krosigk had taken Himmler's words very seriously.

"This tiny creature?" von Krosigk replied. "Your claims to her power are nonsense. She is as frail as a child."

Elianna stepped to the side, opening a view between her and the guards. "*Sagunimallutik nal Ingustik.*" Streams of blackness shot from her outstretched hands, rippling across the room and plunging into the torsos of the Führer's protectors. The guards screamed in agony and dropped to their knees. Unlike what Ernst had seen before, they still seemed alive, but whatever she was doing to them was excruciating beyond measure.

The guards dropped their hands and looked up toward the ceiling, all apparently seeing the same apparition that left them in speechless horror.

The four guards from outside came rushing in, but Himmler stopped them from firing on Elianna. "You will just spend your lives in wasted service," he told them after ordering them to lower their weapons.

Elianna released the guards from whatever torment she'd brought them. They dropped to the floor, two wept, one curled into the fetal position and scraped his face repeatedly against the carpet, the last one rose to his feet and charged through the four newcomers at the door.

They, thankfully, let the fleeing guard go. He appeared to be deserting, but Ernst blamed him not one iota.

"What have you done to them?" von Krosigk asked her, incredulous.

He was too stupid to even be afraid. Ernst wanted to sigh loudly and say as much, but the want wasn't worth dying for.

"What I will do to you and your…" she looked at Frau von Krosigk, "wife if you ever deem yourself worthy of touching me again."

The Führer looked at Ernst, furious. "Did you explain to her who I am?"

Ernst stood up and snapped to attention. "I did, Herr von Krosigk. She is not interested in such knowledge of our society."

"Why have you brought her here?"

"I was ordered to do so, mein Führer!"

"I had no idea how dangerous she is," the Führer lamented. He looked back at Elianna. "Are you here to kill me?"

"What?" She laughed out loud. "No. I'm here to offer my assistance to you, but I'm not sure I'm interested now…"

"What assistance?" von Krosigk asked.

"It doesn't matter," Elianna spat out angrily, her demeanor changing in a flash. "You have gone too far insulting me."

"No!" the Führer bellowed. "You came to negotiate; we will come to a consensus."

Ernst had to begrudgingly admit that at least von Krosigk wasn't a coward. He'd seen the nightmare and was still willing to engage.

"Well then," Elianna said, looking over and smiling at Ernst. "Let's discuss what you want and then we can discuss what I want."

Ernst shook his head so subtly that probably only he noticed. Elianna had never intended to just talk. She'd planned to show von Krosigk her power all along. Because seeing is where real believing comes in.

And now the Führer was a believer.

Judging by the silent demeanor and look on Frau von Krosigk's face, she too was a believer, and just as afraid as Ernst about where it was all leading.

Chapter 5 - Sergeant Nelson

July 14, 1940

"Get that wire in place or we're wasting our time here," Sergeant Johnny Nelson yelled at his men. "You know the drill! We ain't done by sundown, we retreat. Then we take this patch again tomorrow!"

"We're working as fast as we can," Private McKinney shot back.

"Shut up, McKinney, I ain't in the mood. Get this done, because I'm sick of having to fall back every damned day because of lazy SOB's like you."

The private scowled but reached into the trailer with his gloved hands to drag out more wire. Two more men grabbed the bundle and started processing it. Once the men cut the baling wire holding the wire tightly wound, the coil of concertina wire was dragged into position.

Nelson walked away to inspect the previous section the men had put in place. "Give me lip, you little…" he mumbled as he chewed the stub of his cigar.

For some reason, if the soldiers sealed the area behind the wire with one continuous band of metal, the deaders no longer wanted into the area. If there was a gap, or if they didn't clean the bones of the deaders they put down for a second death earlier that day, tomorrow it would be full of the horrors once more. Horrors that would either rip a man apart or cage him in and force him away from the safety of the American line.

Nelson's squad was on their fourth day of duty. Everyone had questions, and few had any answers about what was going on.

As the squad sergeant he'd had a week of instruction and training, but the other squad members were expected to learn on the job.

So far the process wasn't working that great.

"Why don't we just burn all of France like we burn the areas we're securing?" Corporal Wilcox wondered out loud.

"They don't make that many petrol spraying planes," McKinney replied.

Kid was probably right.

Nelson hadn't lost any of his men to the deaders yet, but his squad had one of the lowest rates of success for securing new territory, at least for this week. After a month in Brittany the US Army had less than half the region to show for it. At this rate they wouldn't liberate France before 1952.

Mysteriously, they hadn't found even one French citizen, dead or alive.

"Why doesn't whoever is killing the living and raising the dead send one of those dragons that attacked Berlin to do us in?" Wilcox asked. "That would end our time here real quick."

"Because this is the Devil's work and he ain't none too smart," Private Fensten said, finally giving his two cents.

Nelson rolled his eyes. "The Devil is plenty smart. If you need to believe he isn't smart to get your work done, you believe that for now. But Satan has a plan and he's no fool."

As long as his boys worked hard and got back behind the lines before the deaders surged up once again, they could say about whatever they wanted. But if they slacked, spoke ill of Christians, back talked him or got sloppy in their work, they'd deal with him.

"It's always the Devil with you, Fensten," McKinney said derisively. "If God is all powerful, then how does that Devil of yours get anything done?"

"Quit your blasphemin'," Nelson warned. "I ain't havin' it."

Nelson knew McKinney thought he was some sort of scientist, and maybe he thought he was an atheist, but let a deader get close enough and that would change. If there ain't no atheists in foxholes, then there sure as Hell ain't any around this supernatural evil either.

Nelson carried a Bible in his second holster. On his right hip sat a Colt 1911, and on the left a travel Bible his momma gave him when he left Kentucky for Fort Dix in 1935. It had kept him sane during basic training, and it would keep him sane now. And hopefully provide some of God's protection.

A pair of crop dusters rattled in from the south. They'd drop latex infused gasoline to soak and burn the land to the east for tomorrow's efforts at reclamation. The first of many, soon the sky would be glowing orange and black with smoke. Only the USA was using this tactic as far as Nelson was aware, but probably because only the USA had oil to burn. The Krauts might act up and break their truce at any time, those Nazis were none too reliable. Britain was reportedly stockpiling fuel for any such contingency, ready to fuel their tanks and planes. They didn't trust the Germans either. So, thanks to the bountiful oilfields of Texas, Americans were the only army on the coast of France trying to make a difference.

The dusters looped back and forth no more than a half-dozen football fields away as they soaked the area with fuel from just a few feet off the ground.

Finally, he tore himself away to check in on his men. "Come on, boys, we ain't getting younger. Let's wrap this up and get back behind the lines. If this area isn't full of new deaders for us to kill tomorrow, then we'll move on to the next patch."

A biplane approached, following in the trail of the two crop dusters. A small incendiary dropped over the side of the open cockpit. A flash of white phosphorus and the entire 'dusted' area flashed into a raging fire. A farmhouse and a barn were soon adding to the firestorm. Trees lost their leaves then turned to ash as grassy fields burned away to nothing.

Tomorrow the fire would be out and there would be a new square of gray earth, filled with the dead who surged west toward the Americans every night. The soldiers would fire their weapons from the safety of the ground taken yesterday until none of the dead moved, then the cleanup would begin. Dozers from the combat engineers pushed the dead into rapidly dug pits where they were burned, and their ashes buried once more.

Hopefully to stay this time, because a few times Nelson noticed the pits from the night before turned into churned up earth as the dead escaped to roam again.

He shuddered. They might retake France from the horror that held it now, but what would it be worth? Paris was reportedly filled with the deaders according to aerial recon. Would the military burn the entire city? Where had the Parisians gone? Scuttlebutt was there weren't enough deaders to account for all the people.

A noise from behind the lines caught his attention. He looked at his watch. The truck to pick them up was approaching. The men were as done as they were going to get. "Get ready for the truck, boys. It's time to run away again and hope the line holds."

They'd survived another day. "Hopefully they'll have a good mess tonight," Fensten said. "The ashes of the dead don't taste the best."

"They taste like grit and despair," Nelson replied. He'd gotten used to it already, but he'd been here longer. Every day he and his team breathed in the remains of WWI soldiers, the ashes of French civilians, the burned land, and the remains of farm animals destroyed by the dead. They were still trying to ignore the taste and smell, but it got to them. Every day they hoped for a good meal when they got back behind the wall that crossed the peninsula, one that would finally get rid of that taste. At least overnight.

So far the chow had been adequate. It wasn't that hard to get hot meals and smokes to the battalion, since they weren't moving at any speed that would stretch a supply line and the German U-boats weren't sinking any ships, at least not for the moment. There were reports of some ships not making it, but that had to be the nonsense soldiers said to convince themselves that others have it worse than they do.

He looked around at his squad. Wilcox was technically his second in command, but the kid was twenty years old. And about as mature as an eighth grader. Nelson, with a cigar in his mouth, a flask of whiskey in his pocket, and two days of facial hair was the old man in the unit.

At twenty-four.

"When we get back behind the wall, you all need to check the boards at the command tent and see if you have guard duty," Nelson told the boys. "If you do, you're first in line for food then grab a nap."

"You ever get guard duty, Sarge?"

"Every day I watch you guys like your momma," Nelson answered. "We're not going to lose anyone to stupid if I can help it. I need to be awake for that."

"It's not that dangerous," McKinney replied. "The dead are… well, dead again by the time we come out in the truck, and they don't return that day for some reason."

"You've seen the ones in the trees, no more than a mile away?" Wilcox asked.

"Yeah. They just stay there."

"They're just lulling you into a comfort," Wilcox told McKinney. "You let your guard down, and they will be on you. They can move fast."

"If you say so," the private replied. "I just haven't seen it."

Wilcox started to respond, but Nelson stopped him.

"The second day I was here one got through the fence right after we moved it east," Nelson said. "They're fast alright. Killed three men before the guards could put it down."

The kid looked like he didn't know how to respond.

"I never lie," Nelson said. "I don't break the commandments. Carelessness out here will get you killed," Nelson added. "And that ain't happening on my watch. I see you messing around, and you'll have guard duty every night. If you ain't paying attention anyway, it might as well be 'cause you're tired."

Eyes around the truck widened a bit. Guard duty didn't get a man out of working the next day to clear the land. It just got him exhaustion. A week of it would wear even a young man down.

The rest of the ride was quiet. The boys were nearer to figuring out what sort of sergeant he was. The kind that didn't take to a private doing a thing that wasn't in the soldier's manual.

Nelson crossed his arms and chewed his cigar. He was finally satisfied that this group was smart enough to work with.

As they passed the gate and the door closed behind them, gunfire erupted from the ramparts of the wall.

The deaders were coming once more, trying to take the land back.

"Not today," Wilcox whispered.

"What?" Nelson asked him.

"They didn't get us today."

Chapter 6 - Lost Hold

Irsu Cragstone embraced his wife, Kordina, when she met them at the gates. The engineers had opened the main gates to the Swiss countryside now that the Swiss were allies. It made coming home feel much more like a proud moment than a house burglary.

"You got wounded," she noticed.

"Scratched," Irsu replied, frowning at the thought of her worry.

"He got shot by the Grays," Coragg said. "A bullet almost took the *Amblu-gane's* head clean off."

"You talk too much, Coragg, you're relieved," Irsu said. "Go hit a tavern. I'll see what we're up to next."

"I'll go with you to the tavern…" Numo said, looking cautiously at Kordina.

"What do I care, you oaf?" she snipped at the scout. "Get to drinking, Irsu is staying with me."

"But there will be drinking, right?" Irsu asked.

"You and I are going to go drink my cousin's stock," she said as she grabbed his hands and led him away from the troops that had brought him home.

"Well, at least the liquor will be good," Irsu sighed. "He probably wants me to deliver *schokolade* to Hagirr or something."

Kordina shook her head. "No such thing. It's worse than that."

"I was joking," Irsu protested.

"And I am not. Off to the royal chambers." She dragged him faster. "The Underking awaits his *Amblu-gane*."

"I'm still not comfortable with that title," he complained.

"That makes it all the more fun to say."

When they got to the royal fortress within the hold, they were rushed in without any formality. Irsu knew then that the matter was serious. Most dwarves loved their ritual displays. While Irsu would prefer life uncomplicated and full of simple honesty, his people were renowned for making a one-hour event into an all afternoon display.

"Good," was the only announcement. "You're finally here." From King Scorriss Bloodbane himself. "Where's Numo?"

Irsu bowed to his king, which earned him a look of annoyance. "I sent him and Coragg to the tavern hall," Irsu said. "They've worked hard, the trip was long, and whatever the issue is here they'll be more than happy to go along with anything the clan needs."

"Good dwarves, those two are," the Underking replied. He poured Irsu and Kordina a drink to match his own. "Good to see you, cousin," he said to Kordina as he handed her a mug of wine.

"And you, as always."

Irsu took a deep drink before he spoke. "Why, my king, did you call me away from command?" he kept his eye contact as the King turned to face him. "What is more important than dealing with a people who want to drive us out of our hold?"

"Where would we go if they succeeded?" the King asked. "That question is why you are here."

"Through the gate, back to our old hold, then life would continue as before."

"Two weeks ago, a band of dwarves, in unmarked leather armor, attacked Iron Mountain Hold. They didn't have the equipment to break down the walls and gates, so they didn't get in. The contingent I left to guard the gates held, with only three casualties."

"What clan would dare attack us?"

"That's the thing," the King replied. "They had no markings. No banners. No honor."

Irsu stared at the symbol of Ekesstu on the wall behind the King. No dwarf could be without honor in such a way. They would have no entry into the afterlife.

"Our banners define us," Irsu whispered, in awe of the concept the King had just shared with him. "We are the symbols of our clan, of our gods."

"Not these dwarves," King Scorriss replied. "To make matters worse, they appeared sickly. Pasty skin, eyes so pale they were almost white. The pink inside their eyes reflected back to the torches of our guards."

"Dwarves don't get sick like that either," Irsu said.

King Scorriss frowned, his eyebrows furrowed.

"Except that you say they do and my King speaks the truth in all things," Irsu rapidly added.

Kordina gasped and started to tell Irsu to mind his words.

The Underking held up a hand to stop her and sighed. "Don't worry, I wouldn't believe me either."

"I didn't mean it that way," Irsu answered. "Just the opposite in fact." He put his closed fist over his heart. "What is your command, my king?"

"I want you to go back into the old world. Take a small contingent of soldiers, whatever you need. Gear, weapons, take it from the royal armory. Find these dwarves and get answers. If their disease is infectious, you'll need to stay away from the clan for some time until we see if you've contracted the illness. But you can leave runes outside the gates to Iron Mountain Hold to let us know what you find. If you're not sick in a year, return to us."

"A year?" Kordina exclaimed. "Scorriss! He's my husband, we've but barely married."

"I know," the King replied.

"It's fine," Irsu said to Kordina. "We're not going to get a disease, and what's a year to us? We have centuries. You waited four years while I trained."

She smiled weakly. "I did. That was long enough."

"I'll be back," Irsu told her. He walked to her and pulled her close. "I'll bring you something from the old world. Something we can remember that world by."

"One year," she whispered to him, tears falling into her

beard. "One year."

"No more if this soul can help it. The gods might have other plans, but I don't."

"Take tonight to spend with your wife in your quarters," the Underking told him. "Kordina, he's the *Amblu-gane*. He has to be the one."

She practically growled her response. "Stupid tradition anyway."

"But it's our tradition," Irsu told her, stroking her hair. "Tonight. Then we celebrate in a year. And we're wasting time. Let's go home."

"Go. Go!" Scorriss told them, waving toward the door. "I'll send Coragg for you in the morning."

Irsu held Kordina's hand as he led her to their home.

Chapter 7 – Allies

Harry stood with Miller watching the latest group of Dek leave their summer grounds. In groups of forty or fifty, a few families banded together. Enough for security, but not so many that if a group was destroyed the tribe would be seriously harmed.

A hard pragmatic thought in a hard and brutal world. He hadn't seen a lot of the brutality yet, but from the stories the Dek shared he needed to brace himself.

"What are we doing, Lieutenant?" Miller asked him.

"We're leaving last, Cylethe's orders," Harry replied.

"She's in charge now?"

Harry sighed. He was walking a tightrope. He couldn't surrender his command to this dek, Cylethe. But he did need her knowledge if his men were to survive this world. A very fine tightrope indeed. "I'm in charge, Miller. She is more of a guide, and a smart leader doesn't throw the wisdom of a good guide away."

A dek ran out of the tree line several hundred yards from the edge of the village. The Undek apparently took clearing any new growth around the village as a serious obligation when they returned here each year. Thanks to that diligence Harry's line of sight was considerable.

The dek waved his arms frantically.

"Miller get the unit on alert. Bring the Hotchkiss gun. You're my loader, Tim's already away." Harry pointed to a spot east of their position. "We're setting up on the edge of town. Meet me there. No delay, chap."

"Aye," Miller turned and ran toward the unit's *yoglik*.

No more than two minutes later and the dek runner was in town. Harry and Miller were setting up the Hotchkiss facing the point where the runner had exited the forest. He didn't know what was going on, but the dek was frantic and now the remaining villagers, probably less than five hundred, were frantic as well.

"Damn, I need Parker's amulet."

"The amulet is with Timothy, Lieutenant."

Harry smiled. "That's right. Good of Parker to loan it to him without a mention to me." He pointed at the spot to deploy the Hotchkiss. "Let's get with it."

He hurriedly explained to Miller his expectations for a loader. Several dozen warriors sprinted out of the village and into Harry's line of fire as a shadow darted over the machine gunners.

"NO!" Harry yelled, as he frantically waved the warriors aside "Get out of my way!"

The shadow was Cylethe, flying on some creature that looked more dead than alive. She was quickly over the forest, circling, looking for something.

Suddenly, everyone in place, the scene fell silent.

"I wish I knew what was going on," Miller whispered.

"We need to move," Harry told Miller, then barked orders to all of his men. "Squad! Crossfire formation, end of the Undek lines. As practiced!"

Five men ran left, five, including Miller and Harry, ran right. “Set up just like we did before.”

Miller nodded, doubling his speed as he prepared the Hotchkiss squad gun for action. They kept their center pivot point on the spot the runner had exited the forest. Harry sat down on the ground, raised the rear stock support as Miller splayed the bipod legs and attached the swivel.

The creature Cylethe flew, which he would later learn was a *drakon*, screamed then reared its neck back. Billowing green clouds of thick fumes spewed from the *drakon's* mouth, far heavier than the air it dropped through.

Inhuman screaming erupted from within the trees, letting Harry know there was dying going on.

He found out what a moment later. Beings — very disturbingly different from the horses they marginally resembled — erupted from the tree line and charged across the clearing. Four pumping legs and a human shaped torso, they had two arms and a head. The head was far more like that of a wolf than a person. The centaurs, for lack of a better word, carried spears, shields, and swords as they raced toward the outnumbered dek warriors. Painted symbols decorated torsos and flanks.

Harry charged the Hotchkiss, driving the first round into the chamber. He took a general look down the sites toward the targets, then fired. The gun raised a cloud of dust as gas ejected from the end of the barrel and disturbed the ground ahead, which rapidly blew away to the right of their position.

He shot three round bursts, his years of practice and skill helping him to save ammunition. As the 11mm bullets slammed into the horse-like bodies, they lost footing and tumbled. The stricken beings would entangle the legs of their comrades, taking down more of them. Much like horses, legs often broke during the cartwheeling that followed a centaur going down.

"*Sek-nook*!" the dek nearest him said, smiling and drawing a finger across his throat. Harry knew the meaning of *nook*. Horse. *Sek-nook* must be the name of the creatures.

Later he'd learn the meaning of *sek*. Together they meant half-horse.

The dek set long spears into the ground, pointed toward the charging beasts, a defense Harry judged to be wholly inadequate for the task that needed to be done.

Cylethe's *drakon* took her over the battle, where streaks of energy often jetted down from her hands toward the ground. Occasionally an arrow would rocket up toward her from the rear of the half-horse cavalry. The usual result was the missile stopping in mid-flight as if it hit a wall.

"Red flare," Harry ordered Miller.

Miller, having just reloaded another magazine into the top of the Hotchkiss, pulled out a flare gun and loaded it. The private shot into the air and almost immediately the other riflemen in Harry's squad opened up. He turned back to the task at hand and began the slaughter once more.

Not quickly enough. A dozen or more of the half-horses managed to get past the crossfire and slammed into the lines of the Undek warriors. Some impaled themselves on the long spears, but several slid past, slashing with swords or stabbing with spears. Several dek went down, but others dropped their spears to jump at the half-horses with a seemingly insane commitment to the goal of slaughtering a dangerous enemy.

When a half-horse proved vulnerable the Undek climbed all over the stricken beasts, who seemed to think they were invincible until they realized they weren't. As knives plunged into the creatures, Harry noticed the native warriors never attacked the torso. The guttural growls of the half-horses didn't send a message of fear when the dek took one down. It sounded like hate.

He looked over at Garrett. The loud, staccato pops of the MAS rifle came in rapid succession. The soldier was firing fast enough that ammunition concerns popped into Harry's head. "Garrett, tell the other riflemen on both ends of the line to aim only for the horse part and to preserve cartridges where they can!"

Garrett stopped firing, nodded, and began sharing the order with the man next to him.

Harry opened fire again as a second wave blasted from the forest. This time he put one or two round bursts into the beasts, with the same effect. He had to save ammunition, there weren't any 11mm depots that were going to resupply him.

"Seventh belt," Miller told him. "We have six more."

Damn. There was nothing for it. The creatures had already proved their ability to butcher the dek if Harry did nothing.

The bam-bam of the bursts going off combined with the slow rate of fire for the Hotchkiss made it easy to count the rounds left. Thirty in a belt disappeared all too fast.

"Ninth belt," Miller said.

Still some of the half-horses got through. They mindlessly

threw themselves on the spears. A few charged toward the Hotchkiss and Harry's riflemen, but the men would concentrate on those and none made it through. At least at first. One particularly tenacious example lunged toward Harry and Miller, and only after what had to be a dozen shots or more did his legs fold below him. The creature slid to a stop just in front of the machine gun, spraying dirt all over the Hotchkiss as well as Harry and Miller. The scent of blood, sweat, and intestines was strong.

Sand filled the mechanism of the gun. It had to be cleaned to be fired again or it would be destroyed. "Miller, to your rifle," he said as he pulled his pistol.

Miller joined the other men to Harry's right, firing from the kneeling position. Harry dove on top of the half-horse's prone body to give himself a steady firing platform. He had six shots in his revolver, which he'd been saving for himself and his men to be honest. Somehow the thought of being captured by these creatures frightened him more than the Nazis.

The loud pop of his service revolver had an entirely different sound than the Hotchkiss. And a lot less range. He was unable to shoot the distant creatures, and the ones closer still took two or three shots to bring down. After three reloads he finally clicked on an empty chamber as a half-horse wobbled — then fell in front of him.

The sword the creature dropped was of a size Harry could use. Harry picked it up, then jumped onto the body of the creature that had disabled the Hotchkiss. Two of the men to his right were fixing bayonets to their MASs. Miller and Garrett still had rounds, but probably not many.

Once the last bullets were gone, they'd join the Undek in a last stand with hand to hand weapons. He looked over at the dek.

They had close to a hundred warriors when the fight started. Now there seemed less than half that.

He heard Miller's rifle click empty.

Harry raised his sword and the men around him grabbed spears and swords as well.

"For England!" he yelled, although that made no sense at all. England wasn't even part of this world.

The men charged over the half-horse corpses, which were so numerous the living half-horses were unable to charge in return. They gingerly picked their way through the corpses of their fallen comrades but seemed no less determined to wipe out the Undek villagers.

Miller was next to him when suddenly the private dropped his weapon and jerked fully upright. He arched his back and looked at Harry in desperation.

Then began to change shape.

The private clenched his fist in agony, his jaw moved unnaturally beneath his skull. His lips stretched tight over enlarged teeth and he seemed to be getting taller. Clothing ripped as muscles bent and bones thickened and curved. Harry heard snapping sounds from within Miller's body as changes wracked him.

Cylethe's *drakon* circled overhead. The dek magister leaned over and looked down on Harry and Miller's position. Whatever was happening Harry assumed it had something to do with her.

He had no choice but to hope so, because the battle wasn't stopping for him to tend to Miller.

A half-horse engaged Harry but dramatically underestimated Harry's will to live. It thrust a spear at him, planning to run him through. Harry dodged the point, the wooden shaft slid along his arm tearing his tunic and skin with the scrape of rough wood. Harry swung the sword in his hand at the front knee of the beast, and to his surprise the weapon sheared through the sinewy leg.

The half-horse screamed his rage as he fell.

Harry plunged the sword into the body of the creature repeatedly until its hate-filled eyes ceased to focus. A few moments after that it breathed its last in a spray of foamy blood.

Miller!

Harry turned to look where Miller had been, but the private was gone. A ruckus toward the trees caught his attention. A line of ripped discarded clothing pointed toward the scuffle, Miller's clothing ripped and fallen from his body.

He immediately knew why.

Miller was gargantuan. His features were distorted, but the face of the monster Harry was staring at was still enough Miller that he was recognizable. Except Miller's head was the size of the Matador lorry. He stood nearly fifty feet high. The wicked smile on monster Miller's face increased with each half-horse he smashed.

The half-horses were panicking. Routed, they were fleeing the battle in every direction. Harry estimated that five hundred had arrived, and less than a hundred were fleeing. Mostly thanks to the Hotchkiss and rifles, but Cylethe and the Undek were formidable foes as well.

The *drakon* landed near Harry, then Cylethe dismounted. The

Undek warriors who still lived and were conscious cheered.

"Your doing?" Harry asked, gesturing at Miller, who was chasing down the enemy in seventy-foot strides.

"I asked him first," she protested. "He was eager."

"Fair enough," Harry said, wondering what absurdity this world would bring him next. "It looks like we've won this round."

Cylethe looked around. "No small thanks to you humans. I am grateful."

"As Grandmother said," Harry smiled. "Our people have been allies for a long time."

She grinned. "I believe that now."

"So do I," Harry said.

Chapter 8 – Treaty

Elianna and Ernst were in the back seat of the wheeled transport Ernst called an auto. Whatever the name, it was convenient. It was faster than a horse, but it smelled a lot worse. A chemical scent assaulted her nose whenever she was near one.

"This treaty, you need to take it to your monarch?" Ernst asked her.

"My lover, Hagirr," she informed him. "If your people and my people are to be friends, he will decide. I haven't been as welcomed here as I'd like."

"You are terrifying to those you've met," Ernst said, being frank as she'd asked him to do. "Poor Frau von Krosigk may never be the same."

"Nothing will ever be the same," she told him. "Why should it? Before we arrived, you humans were about to kill each other in huge numbers with your machines. Is this not better?" She didn't wait for him to answer. "You did your people a favor opening that gate, Ernst."

Which was a lie. All humans would be brought through the gate eventually, but if these Germans felt they'd benefit from the process and helped get it done, so much the better.

Ernst looked uncertain. "I can't shake the feeling that Germany isn't exactly in the position of power here."

"Once we're in agreement the dragons will be told to stay out of German territory. The troops that are controlling some of your people right now will retreat to enemy lands and concentrate on the real fight, Ernst. Forcing those without our vision to see it as we do. My world follows the singular vision of Hagirr. Your world will do so as well, and as Germany already does, you will prosper for it."

"You mean my lands and yours are both fascist. Germany will be a puppet of your master?" he asked.

"Hagirr is my lover," she corrected again. "Puppet is a harsh word. The capital of Earth will be in Berlin. Your capital, yes?"

He nodded.

"Germany will make all the decisions except those that Hagirr needs to make," Elianna offered.

"Why should we not fight to retain our independence?"

"Have you not seen enough of my demonstrations to know the answer to that question?"

The look on his face confirmed he had.

"You and Herta are my friends. I will see to it that you are both safe, but I'll need your cooperation if that's going to happen."

"What sort of cooperation?"

"Many humans will have to go through the gate to Aerth and be reeducated there regarding the new order of our worlds."

"This reeducation, it will be with your magic?" he asked.

"If need be." She tilted her head and smiled. "Ernst, you're my lover too. Have you not seen me gentle? Caressing you even?"

He looked uncomfortable. "You can be very attentive."

"And that is how my people think of humanity. A firm but gentle hand is needed. Have I told you that Hagirr is human, as you are?"

"No," Ernst replied. "I thought there were no humans on your world?"

"He has been the only one for ten thousand years, since our worlds were last joined."

"He's not human, then. We rarely live to one hundred."

Elianna laughed, something that seemed to surprise grim and serious Ernst. "I assure you, he's human. As I said, I'm his lover and have been for a long time."

"How's that possible?"

"He's the greatest wizard to ever exist," Elianna replied. "And if you, Ernst, cooperate with our agenda, you and Herta could live thousands of years as well."

That got his attention. Who wouldn't want to live a length of time that seemed to be immortality to a person as short lived as a human?

"Through magic?" he asked.

"Of course. I could speak to Hagirr about a reward for service to the greater cause."

He nodded, then looked forward out the front window of the car. She could tell the thought of centuries of life, or maybe even millennia, pleased him. Such an offer would tug at any being's loyalties.

"We're almost there," Ernst said.

Elianna nodded. Somewhere, high above them, a creature waited to greet Ernst and help her convince the German that cooperation was the path to his success.

The auto pulled onto a dirt path, one which led through a small strip of trees to the edge of a large wheat field.

The driver stopped.

"Let's walk," Elianna said. "It's a sunny day, we can discuss our friendship."

Ernst smiled weakly as he got out. She held all the power, so the German probably wasn't entirely certain it was friendship they shared. He was right, of course, but she had grown fond of him since she'd met him not long ago. He was intelligent, devoid of most senseless morality, and eager to achieve greatness for himself.

All traits she could respect, as she shared them.

They walked for a while in silence, then she took his hand in hers.

"Do you trust me at all, Ernst?" she asked.

"I don't think you'll lie to me unless it's to your advantage to do so," Ernst replied. "I simply need to discern when it's to your advantage to do so."

She laughed. "Clever, and that's why I've grown so fond of you. Intelligence seems to be one of the strong suits of you humans. Hagirr is also brilliant."

"I'm flattered."

"I brought you here to meet someone. You will be afraid. It's normal."

"What?" Ernst asked. "To an empty field?"

A sound caught their attention, they both looked up. One of the mechanical flying machines the humans used was spiraling in a loose circle, almost directly in line with the sun. Because of the glare, it was hard to see. The… aircraft Ernst called them… aircraft plunged to the ground a five-minute walk away.

Ernst broke into a run toward it. She followed.

"An American P-40," Ernst said. "Outdated, slow, not very agile. How could it be here?"

The P-40 was mangled. It had a fanged mouth on the front that gave it the appearance of a cat or dog.

"Is the paint a tribal marking?" Elianna asked.

"No… well, in a sense I suppose. This aircraft would have belonged to a squadron which is sort of a tribe."

Another sound greeted their ears, a whistling then a snap so loud it hurt Elianna's ears. Ernst winced and covered the sides of his head with his hands. She knew what was happening, but Ernst had no idea. Confusion danced on his face.

An immense creature held up a leather wing from the landing spot it occupied just the other side of the crashed aircraft. The wing shaded the sun, prompting Ernst to look up.

He dropped to the ground, crying pitifully. His pants grew darker as wetness spread from his bladder, and he covered his face with his arms.

"I am Rodimikari," the dragon said. "If you had reason to fear me now, your fear would already be extinguished by your death."

Chapter 9 - Iron Mountain Hold

Irsu looked at the gateway that held passage back to Iron Mountain Hold. Each time he saw a gate, it gave him cold shivers down his spine.

A circle of stone, with the blackest of blacks filling the circle. Not a ripple, not a sign there was anything there. Just empty blackness that defied the viewer to see into it. The stone circle, four hands wide on the side, held the magical blackness in place two hands from the edge, directly in the center. From the other side the view would simply be through the ring into the room that held it. The gate was functional on one side, and once a person stuck the first bit of them in, they were committed to the journey.

Without knowing the first thing about what was on the other side if the gate was unfamiliar to them.

A lot of talk was made about how Hagirr's giant gate was the only connection to Earth from Aerth, but it simply wasn't true. It was true, however, that if Hagirr's gate closed, they all closed, and whatever side a person was on was the side they would stay on.

"You cannot go first," Coragg was saying. "I'll go. What if Iron Mountain has fallen?"

Irsu looked at his friend. "And if it has? How would you going first make a difference? I will still not know what has happened on the other side."

"I'd take it back single handedly," Coragg said, a smug look on his face.

"Maybe I should go first," Numo suggested. "I might be the

only one fast enough to dive back through the gate."

"No, I go," Irsu ordered. "Coragg, you follow." He turned to face the other warriors going with them. Twelve of King Scorriss's Royal Guards bedecked in ornate plate armor, tinted copper. Their armor was functional, however, despite appearances. Some of the finest made. Carrying axes, short swords, and crossbows, they were a powerful unit. "You will follow Coragg, in rank order. You will not delay."

"So, I'm last?" Numo asked.

"Don't worry, you'll be first often enough on the other side."

Numo seemed to relax. "At least I'll be able to see where I'm placing my feet."

Irsu grinned. That wasn't far off from his own concern. But there was no cure for it. He turned to face the gate, then charged.

He plunged into a dimly lit abyss with no defined surface to stand on, but an invisible hand guided him toward one of a thousand circular glyphs that surrounded him. A wind blew from the side, and if it was possible for a wind to bear ill intent, this one did. He approached the circle and realized that it was one of the thousands that provided what little light existed in this place between worlds. The glyph was comprised of an uncountable myriad of symbols that danced along the edge of what Irsu assumed was the exit of the gate.

The irresistible hand pushed him through.

Reality once more changed in an instant. He was in a room much like the one he'd just left. Stone, large, ancient. He stood once more on solid ground, his axe at the ready, his feet spread wide in a battle stance. A few dozen dwarves stared at him with their mouths open.

Then they started laughing. “The *Amblu-gane* has arrived!” one bellowed.

“We had no way of knowing what was on this side,” Coragg said from behind Irsu. “You lot of fools shut your beards.” Irsu heard the noise of Coragg sheathing his short sword.

More laughter.

The Royal Guards filed through, followed at last by Numo.

“Who’s in charge at the hold?” Irsu asked the closest gate guardian.

“Hevreg,” the dwarf responded. “She’s in the royal chambers, probably got them barred for extra security. The lass is afraid we’ll be overrun by the diseased dwarves at any moment.”

“What’s the threat level?” Coragg asked.

“The dwarves came to the gate for the East Underway, made a small thrust to get through into the hold, and a lot of them died. Three of ours, shot by bolts through our own murder holes.”

“What did they look like?” Irsu asked the dwarf. “Like dwarves? For certain?”

“They were dwarves, alright. But they have gray skin, eyes almost white, and probably a good two hands shorter than a normal dwarf. Stockier, however.”

“Take me to the bodies,” Irsu ordered.

“Can’t. Hevreg ordered us not to open the gate for two days.

By the time we did, the bodies were gone. Despite constant watch from the side towers, nobody saw them go. They were there, then they weren't."

A chill went down Irsu's spine for the second time in minutes. What the guard reported would require magic. Dwarves willingly using magic of that type? He couldn't help but wonder if their sickness wasn't punishment from the gods for that.

"Then take me to Hevreg," Irsu added.

"Aye, *Amblu-gane*. If she'll let us into the inner corridors."

"Great, just what we need. A royal with a touch of madness locking herself up and away," Coragg muttered.

"We'll hold our judgment," Irsu said. "But if you're right we'll have to change matters here. And right or not, we'll have to solve the mystery of these dwarves."

Coragg nodded.

"Guards, I'm changing your name. You're now the Iron team, in celebration of the company I led to Nollen," Irsu bellowed. "Iron team, guard this gate until I return. I'm off to see Hevreg, and then we'll take a few days to rest, eat, and make a plan. Once we go into the East Underway, we'll be in constant danger. Food will be what we carry with us or find. But we'll need to find the dwarves that attacked Iron Mountain Hold even if it takes a century."

The soldiers started moving to positions they felt would provide the best coverage.

"Also, if I come running back into this room yelling, then get through the gate and defend the other side."

Multiple heads nodded as elite warriors took up positions in the room. They would gladly die to protect the thousands on the other side of the stone circle. Irsu trusted them implicitly.

"I'm ready," he said to the guard he'd been speaking to. "To Hevreg."

Together with Coragg and Numo, he followed the guard into the long corridor that separated the gate from the rest of Iron Mountain Hold. Forever suspicious, the dwarves kept such powerful magic at a distance, with plenty of positions along the corridor from which to defend should the gate be turned against them.

"Ever vigilant we are," Coragg said.

"It's not enough," Irsu replied, his voice sad. "We're still dwindling in numbers."

"Earth will change that," Coragg countered. "I feel it."

"I hope you're right."

Chapter 10 - The Amusement of Dragons

July 15, 1940

Ernst's bladder let go.

Death stood over him. Several stories tall with wings that stretched forever.

The dragon stared at him.

Then something changed. The dragon seemed less threatening and Ernst thought he saw amusement twinkling in the creature's eyes. "This one is particularly fertile with the excretions," the beast said with his deep rumbling voice.

Ernst slowly recovered some of his senses, at least enough to wonder why he wasn't dead yet.

"Elianna, you've made your point," he said, his voice quivering and reduced to a near whisper. "Get me out of this predicament. Please."

"Have I made my point?" she asked, clearly not expecting an answer. "It's important for you to know a few things. This creature that has you laying in a newly formed puddle of your own piss is a servant of Hagirr. Does Germany have anything like this, Ernst?"

"We are a proud nation. You have seen little of it yet." He amazed himself with his own defiance. "And we have fought the dragons and occasionally won."

Elianna laughed, but it was Rodimikari's growl that drove Ernst back into temporary insanity.

"JUST EAT ME AND GET IT OVER WITH!" he screamed.

A few minutes later he realized he was still alive, blind and cowering behind his own arms.

Elianna smiled down at Ernst as she stood over him. "What you're experiencing is called dragon fear. Nobody is going to eat you, at least not today."

"I do not like the taste of human, to be honest," the rumbling voice said in agreement.

When he'd seen the dragons from the reconnaissance plane before, they'd made his stomach quiver even from thousands of feet away. He appreciated even more the bravery of the Luftwaffe and Royal Air Force pilots that were engaging these beasts. There was something primal about the fear the beasts caused, almost as if it was a trait handed down through humanity's past.

"I can't function on the ground like this. If you could hand me something to use as a blindfold I will get up," Ernst told the sorceress.

"Even better," Elianna told him. A second later she was obviously speaking away from his direction. "Rodi, release him from your awe-inspiring fear."

"Done," the deep voice said.

"You can look now," Elianna told him.

He didn't really know if she was trustworthy. Sometimes her sadism was almost childlike, and she'd erupt in laughter over the simplest cruelties. This would fit that situation.

But he had to break the standoff somehow. Slowly he slid his arms apart and away from his eyes. Despite a head the size of a

Panzer III and a brilliant blue eye looking down at him, he didn't feel the insane fear he felt before. Just the normal fear anyone might feel in a similar situation. The same he'd felt before when ordered to commit suicide for the Reich.

He lowered his arms to his side and stood up, trying to remove himself from the wet ground where he'd laid a moment before. Elianna's laughter irritated him, but it wasn't as if he could do a thing about that despite fantasies to the contrary.

"Very funny," Ernst complained.

"This one is somewhat brave," the dragon observed. "Most of the humans, other than their warriors, flee even if I do not have dragon fear raised."

"This one is a warrior," Elianna told her despicable pet. "He's far braver than you'd think a human could be from what the history scrolls told us."

"That's not a hard cloud to top," the dragon replied to her.

"Trust me, Rodi, he's seen some things from me that would make Desert Elves weep into the sand. He's stood tall, if not a bit paler."

"He's somewhat pale now."

"His color will return," she answered. "I summoned you here for a few things. First, to show him what Aerth brings to the table of war. Second, I want you to escort us when we use one of the human flying machines to get to Jangik."

"Jangik is a long flight even for a dragon. These machines can go this far?"

Elianna looked at Ernst.

"*Verdammt*. How am I supposed to know?"

"It is twice as far past the gate as the last time you were seen," Rodimikari told him. "In the window at the bottom of one of your air machines."

"That wasn't you!" Ernst protested. "You're gold colored, that dragon was red."

The creature laughed. "I am the King of Dragons. I see everything, human. I know you watched Koradimarin die over your capital city."

"The purple dragon," Ernst said.

"Yes…" Rodimikari said in such a way that Ernst could tell he was suppressing anger. "Koradimarin. My nephew's mate."

"We defended our cities. What would you expect?"

The dragon was quiet for a while before replying. "You're right, sorceress. This one is braver than most."

"Ernst, can you get us an air machine that can go that far?" Elianna demanded to know.

"The aircraft your friend saw me in before… or another recon aircraft. That is what will have the range to get that far, but maybe not back. That might not matter anyway. There probably isn't a landing strip where you want to go."

"What does that mean?" Elianna asked.

"The plane can land if we can find a flat enough area. Taking off again may be a problem if the ground is too rough."

"I see," she replied. "We will make do."

"I have an idea," Ernst added. "When do we need to travel?"

"I wish to meet Rodi in three days at the gate," Elianna said. "Can we do that?"

"I'm the Director of Ahnenerbe still, since Himmler saw what you are capable of. I should be able to requisition one aircraft on short notice."

"Very well done, Ernst," Elianna praised. "You are making me quite happy that I didn't do something terrible to you when we met."

Ernst swallowed. "Good to know."

"Rodi, meet us at the gate when the sun is high in three days," Elianna told the dragon. "Is that satisfactory? Or do you need more time?"

"There is nothing I cannot do," the dragon bragged. "The question is whether or not I want to do that. I have another task the high elves have asked of me."

"Hagirr will punish your kind again if you fail me," Elianna warned, her voice turning darker.

The wind blowing through the nearby trees was the only sound Ernst heard for several minutes. The hate summoned into the dragon's eyes was hard to mistake for anything else.

Finally, as wings swept upward for the beast to take off, the creature answered. "I will be there."

A howl of wind and the snap of leathery membranes told Ernst the dragon had taken off. He'd closed his eyes a few seconds earlier, in case the dragon chose to instill fear in him again. Elianna would bring out the worst in anyone. There was no reason a dragon should be an exception.

A full minute later he opened his eyes to look around. Elianna was staring at him scornfully. "You stink."

"Thanks to you," Ernst said.

She laughed at his accusation. "I will summon a water elemental to restore some of your dignity."

For a ten-minute period he got to learn what it was like to nearly drown. Repeatedly. But at least he and his clothes were clean when he got back to the car.

The driver was gone, probably affected by the dragon as Ernst had been. The creature was too big not to see from here.

"Can you manipulate this thing?" Elianna asked him.

"I can."

She laughed her childish laugh. "Then teach me!"

And so a day full of torture that started when Ernst met a dragon continued to torment him as his primary tormentor drove him forty kilometers to Berlin in fits and starts.

Surprisingly, they arrived intact. Or sadly. He wasn't certain.

Elianna returned to her apartment, and Ernst, relieved to have some time apart from her, set to work acquiring one of the seaplanes he'd seen in Hamburg when the *Admiral Hipper* was launched. A seaplane could land on the nearest water to this city Elianna wanted to visit, and then takeoff to come home.

A perfect solution.

Chapter 11 - A Day of Loss

July 16, 1940

The day started much like any other. Sergeant Johnny Nelson sat in the mess tent with his men. His squad and two other squads were in the third rotation for chow, which meant they'd get out on the front to put wire in place over an hour after the first group of squads. The food generally started to turn into pig slop by the time the third rotation ate, and it was even worse on fourth rotation which was tomorrow. But since everyone returned to the safe zone at sunset, it meant an hour less work.

One of life's many trade-offs.

"How'd you sleep, sarge?" Private McKinney asked, sitting down across from him.

"Like one of God's blessed children," Nelson replied. If by blessed he meant with a restless soul that hadn't slept a full night since leaving the family farm.

"Wilcox says you don't sleep much."

"Corporal Wilcox should mind his own business," Nelson said as he bit into a slice of limp bacon.

"I told him I think it's because you like us more than you let on and worry we're going to be deader food."

Nelson scowled at McKinney. "Private McKinney should see to his own business too."

The kid shrugged and shoved some gelatinous scrambled eggs onto a piece of toast.

The bite never made it to his mouth. Sirens went off.

"Squad, get your rifles," Nelson ordered. "Form up in front of our tent. Grab something to eat and bring it with you."

The men scrambled. Nelson grabbed the four remaining strips of bacon on his plate, put on his hat, and headed for the door.

Outside the camp was in chaos. Smoke streaked across the sky, and gunfire erupted from the barrier wall that kept the deaders away. The strong pulse of .50 cal machine guns tapped at his ears.

"Somethin's mighty wrong," he muttered as he shouldered his M1. He'd sent off some letters to his family yesterday. At least they'd get a final word if this was it for him.

A whistling sound overhead caught his attention and he looked up. An M2 tank tumbled downward toward the ground. As he watched a body flew out from the main section of the tank. Probably the driver slipping out of his viewport hatch.

The tank slammed into the ground and rolled, obliterating a line of tents that included Nelson's squad.

"No!" he growled as he ran toward the carnage.

In the distance, from the other side of the barrier wall something growled back, a deep rumble that stirred a sense of doom in Nelson's heart.

A second tank, whistling and shrieking as it sliced through the air the same as the first, flew in a ballistic arc before it slammed into a different part of the camp a few hundred yards away. There weren't any tanks deployed with Nelson's section of the line, so he had no idea where they were coming from. Or what sort of enemy could hurl a tank into the US defensive lines.

Nelson arrived where his tent used to be. McKinney and Wilcox stared blankly at the torn fabric and smashed bodies of their comrades. A huge divot in the ground reeked of fuel, likely from the tank which now lay another six tents down on its side. Blood seeped from the downward facing machine gun port on the turret, the main gun buried in the soil.

"Was everyone in there?" Nelson asked.

"Everyone sarge," McKinney said, "except me and the Corporal. After you said to get moving, we moved. The others were slower."

"They were still in the tent gearing up," Nelson finished. "Dammit," he said then spat on the ground.

Where were the officers with a plan?

The guns on the barrier were still firing, but less of them now. Even as Nelson finished the thought an explosion rocked the wall, opening up a section.

"We are screwed," Wilcox said.

Nobody was directing the men. Nelson needed to think of something. "Both of you are with me. We're going to gather up the lost souls around here and get ourselves into a fighting force once more."

"What do you want us to do?" McKinney asked.

Nelson looked at the tent. If there was rifle and ammo in there, the rifles were probably mangled, and the ammo scattered.

"First thing is, if we see anyone that looks lost, get them with us. I'll do the same. The second is we grab every weapon and ammo pile we see, even if it's just one bullet."

"Got it," Wilcox said. "Where are we going to go?"

"We'll head away from the line at first. Us three can't fight something that's tossing tanks at us. If we get enough men together, we'll make a stand."

Two Curtiss P-36s roared overhead, flying toward the dead zone. Nelson doubted they'd return if what was going on in the encampment was any indication.

"I found a box of bullets!" McKinney exclaimed.

"Just stuff 'em in your pockets," Nelson ordered. "We'll count them later and the last thing I need is a running report." He noticed a young man standing, in his underclothes. "Where's your tent, kid?"

"Smashed. I was at the showers," he answered.

"Bad day for your shower day," Nelson said. "Grab some clothes and follow us. It looks like a total loss here."

Equipment rained down on the camp. Tanks, the trucks that carry the wire laying troops to their duties, and even a few old French cars. Part of a house and some furniture. Then a tree.

What would fight like that?

"What's your name?" Nelson asked the kid.

"Lieutenant Eads. Terrance Eads."

Great. An officer.

"I see what you're thinking, sergeant," Eads said. "Far as I'm concerned, you're in charge. I have no idea what's going on here."

"Good man, sir. I don't either, but I might have a few years on you." Nelson waved at his two remaining troops. "Boys, let's find the L-T some clothes if we can. Don't be picky."

Ten minutes later the group had grown to eight, and the lieutenant was dressed in a mix of clothes found scattered from destroyed tents.

"You, what's your name?" Nelson demanded of one of the new guys, a red headed boy who looked like he could carry a tractor.

"Billy."

Apparently, Billy didn't have a rank anymore, but Nelson didn't have time to care. "Billy, you're my mule. We're going to stack you up with things we might need once we decide we're going to fight."

The big man just nodded.

A sound overhead told him there was incoming. Three of the new guys were smashed under a flying tree trunk. The L-T was one of them. Billy screamed like a seven-year-old girl.

The sheer volume of material raining into the American lines was making it hard to stay alive. Vehicles weren't dropping in anymore, but now it was rocks that looked as if they'd been pulled from the very ground under the French fields.

"We need to move faster," Nelson ordered. "Finding

materials is secondary, I want us double timing away from the line. If we stay here, we're all dead."

"Isn't that desertion?" some kid Nelson didn't know asked.

"You can stay if that suits you," Nelson told him. "I don't have time to make you follow my orders. But I'm US Army property and I'm no good to anyone dead."

To punctuate Nelson's point a scream so loud it was audible over the gunfire and carnage pierced the air.

The kid looked toward the scream, then with a panicked face back at Nelson. "I am US Army property too, sergeant. I should probably come along."

"Good. Now keep your eyes open, and grab what we can use."

A thumping sound was the next nightmare. A rhythmic cadence of deep wingbeats that kicked Nelson's sense of dread into overdrive. Fearing what he'd see, he looked back toward the line. A dozen dragons, still distant, dotted the sky.

"We need to get to cover," Nelson barked. "I know the place, follow me."

He led the ragtag squad to a road that ran southwest, weaving from town to town along the peninsula. A quarter mile ahead was a bridge, made of concrete and solid. If they could get that far, they might have cover from the sky.

"Run." Nelson picked up the pace, and even Billy seemed to understand the urgency as they ran. The giant kid clattered like a drumset as he ran along, bags and ammo draped across his person.

Two minutes later they were climbing off the road into a small ravine and up under the bridge. Just as the dragons crossed the barrier wall.

Nelson's head barely poked above the grass as he looked back east. The creatures dove lower and began strafing the American line. Fire he recognized, but some of the dragons seemed to use different weapons as they shot death from their mouths. One had a cone of electricity. A line of men shooting at the beast convulsed, turned black, then died as their skin burned.

He felt a sense of shame inside, along with a sense of relief. Those men had stayed to fight, but, on the other hand, Nelson and the young men he had under the bridge with him were alive to fight another day. He wasn't sure anyone else would be after the mauling he was observing.

Near the wall, almost two miles away now, Nelson saw a host of men on horses. White horses, with pennants flapping in the wind on long poles. The dragons left them be. They might look angelic on their white horses, with their long hair and elegant weapons… but Nelson saw them for who they were… agents of Satan. He climbed a bit higher above the grass to get a better view. He counted them. Twelve. Of course there were twelve.

"Sarge, they'll see you!" McKinney complained, fear dripping from his voice.

He was right. Nelson dropped a bit lower. If he could see the horsemen, they could potentially see him.

"We need to know how they fight," Nelson explained. "Get back under the bridge and stay there. I'll observe, and if they look to be heading this way, I'll be right there with you."

Normally Nelson would have told him to shut up and do his job for questioning orders, but today was rife with special circumstances. The kid deserved to know why Nelson was taking a risk.

The dragons strafed the American line with incessant fury. Fuel dumps exploded, tents burned, vehicles melted into slag. He was glad he and the other survivors didn't grab a truck to make their escape.

It was over in minutes, at least along this section of the barrier wall. Smoking ruin and slowly dying fire was all that was left of the US Army. The dragons flew wider from the barrier and Nelson took refuge with his new squad.

"What did you see?" some kid asked.

Nelson didn't want to demoralize them to the point they wouldn't act, but they needed to know where they stood.

"I just saw us lose this battle," he told them. "We're not falling back to make a new line and fight. After what I just saw, we might be all that remains alive. Our goal is, God willing, to stay that way."

"The deaders will get us," one lamented.

"Maybe they will." Nelson pulled his Bible from his holster. "But this guy has always been on America's side. When evil seems to have the upper hand, that's us being tested. Rise to the call, fight for what's right, and we will win."

Three of the men reached out and touched the Bible, and Nelson could see the tension pour from them like water from a pitcher. He extended it closer to the others, and they too, even if they had doubt in their souls, caressed the cover.

"This," Nelson said, waving the Bible in his hands, "is the core of our unit now. We fight for God and country to survive, to get somewhere to tell our tale so the leaders of our country can find a way to defeat the evil that has set upon us."

"Amen," the men said.

Chapter 12 – Migration

The Undek were kind in showing their appreciation for the efforts of Harry's squad. After the battle with the half-horses, they were out of ammunition except for a few rounds. He needed to send a team to the Matador to recover all the remaining ammunition and supplies. The dek had given them pack horses for the purpose, along with a host of supplies they could probably not actually spare. But gratitude was gratitude, and if tomorrow is tough that's acceptable if one survived today.

All it had cost the infantrymen was half their ammo supply.

"We're going to need to learn to use the traditional weapons of this place," Harry told Miller. "I'm putting you in charge of the resupply run. Make sure you grab the dwarven weapons we recovered and the ammunition for them."

Miller looked woozy, not having fully recovered from his experience as a giant. Cylethe told Harry it would take a few days, but they didn't have days. He'd given Miller a few hours instead.

"Lars, keep an eye on Miller, and if he can't get the job done then you're in charge."

"Ye kin count oan me," Lars promised.

"Smart move," Miller agreed. "We'll be back in a few hours with the materials."

Harry kept three soldiers with him as well as two of the pack horses. They needed to pack up their *yoglik* and get on with the task at hand. When Miller returned, they'd get on the trail with the still mysterious Cylethe with them.

Packing horses isn't as easy as he thought it would be. And he was a farmer. The balance of the dek pack saddles seemed critical, and the saddles couldn't be overloaded, or the hard leather platform of the saddle would slip off the center of the horse's back. Harry thought of a number of designs that would improve the functionality.

There was no time for improvements, however, and two hours later when Miller returned a quarter of the squad's supplies were on the backs of the men. At least there were six more to share the load with, although many of them were carrying goods from the lorry.

"What a terrible design," Miller lamented to Harry.

"Same thoughts," Harry agreed. "But it looks like we'll be carrying some of our own."

"That's why it's that way," Cylethe interjected. "To respect the animal, to keep unthinking souls such as yourselves from overburdening the poor creatures."

Harry nodded. That was how the dek tended to think.

"Into the *yoglik*, lads, we're leaving our uniforms here."

"What?" a few exclaimed.

"The dek have given us armor and weapons, and they're built a lot like us. They should fit well enough. If we dress like the locals, we'll attract less attention."

The men stared at him. A few of them tugged at their uniforms.

"It's not a request," Harry said.

That was enough. They filed inside and he listened to them grumble as they changed. He moved to the doorway and looked at Cylethe. "Should we expect trouble on the way?"

"Always expect trouble, Harry, you'll live longer," she replied. "But I'll be in your group with a *drakon* as my mount. Only the strongest enemies would dare… or desperately hungry animals I suppose."

"That beast you ride looks dead," Harry commented, finally saying what he'd wanted to say for hours. He'd been afraid of insulting her.

"The *drakon* live on the edge of life and death," she replied. "They see both worlds."

"What do you mean?"

"They're born from eggs that dragon mothers reject from their clutch. The dragons have figured out that they can sell the unwanted for items to increase their hordes."

"You got that," Harry waved at the beast lounging in a grass field at the edge of town, "by bargaining with a dragon?"

"Isn't that what I just told you?"

He shook his head. Just when this world seemed to make any sense, the reality swept it all aside into confusion once more. "And it's part dead?"

"No, it's alive. But it sees into the world of the dead just as you and I see our world."

"Ghosts?" Harry marveled.

"Among other less pleasant things."

The men filed out of the *yoglik* at that point, moving to and standing in a semicircle around Harry and Cylethe.

They actually looked pretty smashing. "My turn." Harry went inside and changed into the armor he'd picked out for himself. He looked at the bassinet helmet that he'd left on his bunk, then decided not to wear it. He kept his infantry helmet instead. That way the men would be able to identify him during the chaos of any battle.

He slung a long sword across his back, not that he knew how to use it.

Stepping back outside, he nodded at his men. "This is me," he told his men, pointing to his helmet.

"You ready to go?" Cylethe asked. "The last of my people departed an hour ago. We are the last in the village."

"More than ready," Harry said as he looked at the now empty *yogliks*. A week ago, the space between the buildings was swarming with activity. Kids playing, merchants, cooks, guards. Now they were empty, and the effect was haunting.

As they marched out of town, Harry on his horse, Cylethe overhead on her *drakon*, and the men walking the pack horses, they passed the dead half-horses. The beasts were too heavy to move, so were left where they lay. Next summer the Undek would return to a field of bones, ready to be made into tools or jewelry.

It was the harsh reality of this world. The weak, even if they believed they were the strong, didn't last long.

Camp that first night was in a place obviously meant for it. A fire ring already in place, the men built a fire and cooked a few chickens they'd gained as reward for saving the tribe. A pot of wild rice simmered, and each soldier had a share of meat and rice for dinner.

They were going to need more food. Hunting was going to be a priority.

"We have rice, beans, and even some potatoes," Harry said. "But if we're going to have meat, that means hunting."

"She could hunt better than all of us together," Garrett said.

"I do not eat animals most of the time," Cylethe said. "My *drakon* is discomforted by the taking of animal life."

"With those teeth? You don't eat meet?" Burke said, grinning.

"Burke!" Harry chided. "Manners."

"Burke is it?" Cylethe asked. "I should say, you're onto something. I don't eat meat unless it's the only choice. I don't hunt animals." She looked at Burke and grinned, baring her teeth. The firelight cast shadows on her face and made her teeth look even more deadly. "But I do hunt, I assure you."

Burke audibly gulped.

"That's enough," Harry said. "My point is that we need to learn to use these bows and crossbows we have. We'll hunt with those."

"Ah cannae skelp a barn wi' they hings!" Lars protested.

Cylethe nodded her agreement. “I suspect he can’t. You humans are weak without your noise sticks.”

“Guns,” Harry advised her. “And you’re right. We’re going to fix that. If you want meat, you’ll learn. I suppose we’ll see how much you want something to eat other than rice and beans.”

The men groaned for a bit, but campfire talk quickly returned to laughter and the sense of brotherhood they’d developed since their first days together. Harry let them talk, even with the topics growing a bit coarse now and then. This was a new world. None of them had to follow him anymore, but they did. A matter of trust and faith, Harry suspected. Something he’d earned, but also something he had to keep alive with his actions.

He’d get them home. He promised himself that much.

Chapter 13 - The King's Sister

Irsu stared at the dwarf before him. She didn't look anything like what he'd expect from the King's sister. Unkempt, eyes darting, the beads in her beard were uneven and mismatched. Her armor was unpolished. He thought he even spied rust forming at the edge of the joints.

"You say my brother wants you to investigate the attack on Iron Mountain Hold?" Hevreg repeated for the tenth time.

She was insane. He had no idea what to do about it. He needed her to see to the defense of the Underway entrances. Could she be trusted to do so when she couldn't even remember a conversation for five minutes? "Yes, princess," Irsu stated. "I'm Irsu Crackstone, Iron Commander and *Amblu-gane* of King Scorriss Bloodstone. He sent me to find where the sick dwarves came from and discover why they attacked."

"Lies!" she screamed. "Arrest these dwarves!"

"It is the truth!" Irsu protested.

Hevreg's eyes burned with insanity, and spittle flew from her mouth as she screamed orders. "Banish them to the East Underway they so wish to see." She pointed in entirely the wrong direction with a shaking finger. "Along with the soldiers they brought with them."

The guards in the royal chamber, the same ones Irsu had stood in after meeting Kordina almost five years prior, lowered their pikes or drew short swords and axes.

"He's the *Amblu-gane*," Coragg protested.

"The King himself ordered that Princess Hevreg was to be obeyed in all things," the guard captain stated. "We can see what's going on here, but there is no choice in the matter."

"I'm beginning to like the way you question orders," Coragg muttered to Irsu.

The guard captain gestured toward the exit. "Come along, we'll see you're on your way."

"GET THEM OUT! GET THEM OUT!" Hevreg was screaming. "TRAITORS! BANISH THEM!"

Did she have the sickness?

The guards led them from the room, and away from the royal stronghold. Once outside the captain was apologetic. "I'm sorry, Irsu, but I have no choice."

"We dwarves have believed we have no choice of our own for far too long," Irsu replied. "You have a choice. You've just forgotten how to make it."

"Easy for you to say," the captain replied. "She hasn't threatened to lop off your head."

A hundred and fifty soldiers escorted Irsu's team to the East Underway. The massive doors had not been opened in half a decade. Thick stone with an ironwood cladding, they were thousands of years old. Five stories tall and probably unmovable without the machinery behind them, a retractable iron bar rested in hoops on the back of both doors.

"What's the status of the Underway?" the captain asked the dwarves manning the tower on the right side of the door. The other side of that tower would look down the passageway from murder holes to scout the situation.

A minute later an answer came. “The East Underway is clear as far as a flaming bolt can shoot.”

A platform several stories off the floor housed the levers and chains that controlled the doors. The guard captain yelled up. “Retract the bar and open the gates!”

“You don’t have to do this,” Numo said to the man.

The Royal Guardsmen in Irsu’s contingent were silent. They probably thought there was no choice either.

“He’s right,” Irsu said. “If I’d followed my orders blindly, I’d not be *Amblu-gane*.”

“If I don’t follow my orders, I’ll not be alive tomorrow,” the response came.

The doors swung open. Moist subterranean air rushed in from the deep highway that appeared before them. A few tenths of a *kadros* away a bolt burned on the floor, flickering flames trying to cling to life as the pitch on the bolt burned away. Shadows danced above it, wreaking havoc with Irsu’s ability to see into the darkness.

The soldiers of the hold lined up to create a living hallway to the door. Several had large bags, and the two who were last in line before the exit held a pack lizard each.

“What’s this?” Irsu asked.

“She said I had to banish you,” the guard captain said. “If you’re the *Amblu-gane* as you say, then I expect you’ll live. These materials might help."

Irsu clasped the captain's arm. "You did what you could. I bear no ill will toward your family."

"I can't hope for more than that."

Irsu looked at Coragg. "It looks like it's an investigation whether we like it or not."

"Life is never boring as your second," the grizzled warrior answered. "What now?"

"In this case there is no choice," Irsu replied. The flaming bolt had expired. He thrust his axe toward the beckoning darkness. "Onward."

The fifteen dwarves marched resolutely in line down the corridor of soldiers. As Irsu's squad passed the soldiers with bags, those soldiers handed them over to the banished warriors. Finally, at the end of the guards, the last two handed over the pack lizards.

"Ekesstu preserve you," one of the last two said to Irsu.

"On your way," the captain bellowed. "You are hereby banished from Iron Mountain Hold unless reprieved by King Scorriss Bloodstone. If you are seen again without such reprieve, you will be tried and executed in accordance with Dwarven Law."

Irsu nodded. He didn't feel like being very noble at the moment to his tormentors.

"You heard the captain," he said to his lot. "On our way."

Chapter 14 - Crossover

July 18, 1940

Ernst thought it ironic that the plane he chose for the flight to Jangik was named the *Seedrache*. The Blohm and Voss BV-138 Sea Dragon could land on water, solving the problem of no runway in Jangik. There was room for the pilot and copilot, three turret gunners, and five more people.

Elianna would be on board, as would Herta at the sorceress's insistence. Of course, he'd be there. That left seats for two soldiers. Ernst contacted Werner von Krosigk, who still had some pleasant thoughts toward Elianna. The young officer assigned guards for the mission, SS troopers who were trained in several forms of combat.

Ernst knew that would do nothing to save Herta or himself if Elianna turned against Germany. But the Germans wouldn't go down without a fight.

Elianna had been tolerable since humiliating him at the hands of a dragon. Not that she couldn't use her own horrible methods, but something about losing his bladder control really irked Ernst. So while Elianna seemed to sense that she'd actually damaged his psyche, he felt less likely to cooperate with her if he could get away with it.

A new noise drew him back to the present. The plane's diesel engines fired up as Ernst waited. Sitting on a trolley designed to be pushed into the water and float the plane, the passengers would get on board first.

"Director, you can board at your leisure," a young lieutenant said.

"*Danka*," Ernst replied, and pushed gently in the small of

Herta’s back to urge her to board.

Ten minutes later they were all on the plane. A truck pumped in the last bit of fuel, departed, and then the plane jolted as a small tractor pushed them toward a ramp into the water. Soon they’d be in the air over Hamburg, and not too long after headed west to the Rotterdam gate.

Rotterdam.

How he wished he’d shot Gustaf Meckler before the fool had the gate open, when Ernst had let the eager fanatic have his way. France would now be German, and probably much more of Europe. Damn Hitler and his lust for power in any form, the occult had thwarted Germany, not helped.

“What are you thinking,” Elianna asked him over the roar of the engines.

“How different life would be if the gate hadn’t opened,” Ernst answered, honestly. He handed her a pair of headphones to wear, then one for Herta. The soldiers were on their own, they didn’t need to hear this conversation anyway. He put headphones on his own ears.

“That’s better,” Elianna said. “Although these are clearly not made for elven ears.” She winced as she adjusted the phones.

“We can talk among ourselves,” Ernst told her. “The pilots will break in to advise us on approach to the gate. Those are their instructions.”

“For once I will sit back and let you run things,” Elianna said, again, unusually agreeable.

“I am both excited and terrified,” Herta blurted out in confession. She was squeezing Ernst’s hands so hard that both her fingers and his were drained of blood and shock white.

“I promise you that you are under my protection,” Elianna swore. “Both of you.”

Ernst wondered if Herta was aware that Elianna was forcing him to sleep with her. Not that it was a terrible burden, but it was hardly worth all the other nonsense he had to bear from the mad elf.

“You told your friend to make sure to turn his overbearing presence off?” Ernst asked Elianna.

“You mean Rodimikari’s fear?” She laughed. “I’m in this flying machine too. Of course I did.”

“Let’s hope he listens.”

“Let’s hope he does,” Elianna agreed. “Dragons can be temperamental.”

“I will be able to look at him without terror?” Herta asked.

“You will have natural fear.” Elianna answered. “But magic will not be the cause.”

That seemed to please Herta substantially.

“Why are we making this trip?” Ernst asked Elianna, staring at her face. “Would it not be easier for this Hagirr to magic himself to us?”

“Hagirr doesn’t inconvenience himself for the likes of a diplomatic visit,” Elianna replied. “That’s my job. And now that I’ve determined your people are worthy, you will meet him in Jangik.

Together we will explain the failure to secure the Ark of the Covenant, as you call it."

Ernst swallowed. That's the first time he'd heard that. Would this Hagirr wish to hold someone accountable? Maybe. He looked at the two SS soldiers. Were they in Ethiopia with Werner's command?

"If he's displeased, these two men are part of the contingency that failed to find it," Ernst said.

Herta started to speak, probably in protest. Ernst squeezed her hand until she exclaimed her pain.

Elianna looked over at the soldiers, who were looking out of their window. She stared back at Ernst, expressionless. Ten seconds later she smiled broadly. "I understand. If it comes to that, I will provide that information."

Ernst nodded at her. At least they understood each other on some level. Elianna needed Ernst, and to a lesser degree Herta since she was Ernst's wife.

For the next hour the three of them exchanged conversation, Elianna learning more about Earth and Germany, Ernst and Herta about Aerth and Jangik. The elf didn't speak about Hagirr, even when pressed.

"Director, we are over the gate," the pilot broke in.

"Start a slow, loose spiral descent," Ernst instructed. "Hold at two thousand meters but continue the spiral if our escort hasn't arrived."

Ernst respected these pilots. They knew a dragon was coming but flew the mission anyway. They certainly could have been unavailable if they wished. But some men wanted to experience things for themselves. These aviators were such men.

Elianna closed her eyes for half a minute, then opened them. "Rodi is nearby. Give him a few minutes."

He blinked rapidly remembering the last encounter. That Elianna had a pet name for such a terrifying monster was an indication of how fearsome she was.

"I see it," one of the pilots said.

"Him," Elianna corrected with a bit of a growl.

"Sorry, madam."

"Follow me," the dragon said outside the plane. The rumble of the beast's voice vibrated the skin of the aircraft, everyone inside heard it… him quite clearly.

"Director?"

"I think you should do as the dragon says," Ernst said into his microphone.

The BV-138 rolled out of the perpetual bank it was in and followed northward. A moment later they were through the gate and instead of a circle of unfamiliar terrain, there was something else. Europe was gone, replaced with a much drier land of scrub and ravines.

"This is the path to take," Rodimikari told them. "If I leave you, straight flying will take you to the wizard. The human. Hagirr."

If Ernst wasn't mistaken, he detected a bit of anger or distaste in the dragon's words. At least from his point of view. Was the dragon an ally of the wizard or a slave? If the latter, that would explain some of the tone and inflection. And it might mean the dragon bore extra animosity for the passengers of this aircraft.

Whatever Rodimikari's feelings, he did as instructed. He led them, during the next few hours, over terrain that slowly grew lusher. Deciduous trees grew below in vast forests.

"The lands of my cousins, the *Askranna'li'anar*," Elianna informed him. "The Wood Elves are a primitive and sometimes violent people. Even Hagirr has left them mostly alone."

Ernst filed the information away. If for some reason they found themselves on the ground, circumvent the forests between Jangik and home.

Trees gave way to a verdant grassy plain, with wide slow-moving rivers. To the north a brilliant blue sky reflected off what appeared to be a sea or ocean. And, in time, a walled city as expansive as he'd expected appeared at the joining of two rivers.

Perfect places to land if this was Jangik.

Elianna confirmed his suspicions.

Ernst watched the city on approach. A horde of people, if that's what they were, noticed the plane. Many surged toward the walls nearest the river.

Great pyramids rose from within the city, as well as extensive stone buildings more beautiful than anything in Berlin. The city glowed white in the sunlight.

The landing was smooth, the river had no rocks breaking the surface, fallen trees didn't litter the currents. The BV-138 pulled up to a shoreline set with square hewn rocks large enough to fish from if locals so wished. Either nobody wished to do so today, or the area was cleared for their arrival. The rocks formed a wall that rose twenty centimeters from the water. The left side wing stretched over the wall as the pilots expertly steered the plane to a spot. To the passengers could step from the plane to the wall without difficulty, making disembarking easy.

After disembarking Ernst took pause as a group of fifty horsemen rode up, all on white horses, pennants raised high. The symbology meant nothing to him. The noise from the plane engines finally died away and Ernst heard the crew preparing to disembark as well.

A single rider dismounted and approached Elianna. An elf, and from what Ernst could tell, of the same race as Elianna. For the first time he heard her speak in her native tongue, with no translation.

It was beautiful. Herta gasped and clutched his hand. Without Ernst or Herta understanding the words, the language struck them like the finest poetry or opera verse.

The two hugged for a long time, the rider was clearly ecstatic to see the sorceress. Something Ernst doubted happened too often.

Elianna turned to the Germans. "Trisari, these are humans from Earth and my guests. Your warriors are to treat them with the same respect they'd give me."

"It is my honor to serve," the male elf said, bowing. "I am Trisari Maltathi Sukihnopinar, Regent of the Guard and Commander of the Jangik Legions."

Ernst grinned a little inside but kept his face stoic. Posturing was the same everywhere. "I am Ernst Haufmann, Director of Ahnenerbe, loyal servant and trusted adviser to Herr Lutz Schwerin von Krosigk."

"Impressive," Trisari said, although he probably had no idea what Ernst was talking about. "Are you a military man?"

"I was until selected for my current position," Ernst replied.

"Excellent. We must talk later over dinner and wine." Trisari turned to Herta. "And you? You have the look of importance on your face. Are you a wizard?"

Herta laughed. "What? Oh, lord no, sir. I am the wife of Ernst, and assistant Director of Ahnenerbe. I am a loyal citizen of Deutscshland and servant of the Führer."

"I see," Trisari replied. He waved back to the riders. "We have horses for you, such important people should not have to walk." He extended a hand toward Herta. "May I assist you to yours, gracious lady?"

Herta giggled, to Ernst's embarrassment. "I would be honored, sir," she crooned as she took Trisari's offered hand.

Elianna grinned at Ernst and stepped closer. "You might not be the only German sleeping with an elf soon," she said quietly, taunting him.

Ernst considered what she said. "Honestly, Elianna, if it makes her happy I don't even care."

"My Ernst is growing up," Elianna said gleefully. She pointed at the city walls nearest them. "Welcome to Jangik, the city of a thousand pleasures."

"I can't wait," Ernst sighed.

Chapter 15 - Étables-sur-Mer

July 18, 1940

Sergeant Nelson rested on a beach. He, and the five men with him, walked two days north to get to the sheltered cove. White sand and a blue sea gently greeted them. Boats bobbed enticingly behind a breakwater. He scanned the sea for signs of shipping, but nothing caught his eye.

He wondered why there were boats still in the marina. Why hadn't the French taken them to seek refuge in England when the dead came?

McKinney plopped down on the sand next to him, for a moment creating a shadow over Nelson. "Sarge, you're going to need to see what we found."

"What did you find, McKinney?" He pointed at the marina and adopted a sarcastic tone. "Dead sailors walking out of the sea?"

"I reckon you could put it that way."

Nelson jerked his head toward the kid. McKinney wasn't joking.

"Really? Dead sailors? I'm tired, and we need to find some food and rest. This ain't no time for jokes."

"We might be fine resting here, I don't know," McKinney said. "That's why I want you to see what we found. Resting here… that's your call, you're the sergeant."

"Show me," Nelson replied, gruffly. He had walked enough, and in two days the only food they'd had were two raw rabbits they'd managed to catch. They didn't dare light a fire to cook it.

Maybe now, in some of the houses of this small commune, they'd be able to cook some good food. Maybe fish a little out on the piers.

McKinney led him east on the beach, then he followed up a trail that climbed the steep cliffs bordering the white sands and blue waters.

"It's one cove over," the private told him.

When they got to the top of the ridge that separated the coves, five of his new squad mates lay prone on the rocky outcrop. They peeked over into the sea and beach northeast of them.

Nelson dropped to the rock and peeked with them. "What're we lookin' at?"

Two ships lay broken on the sand, a British destroyer still flying the flag of the UK, and a submarine of some kind. Both ships were bow first from the sea, plowed deeply into the shore. They were at least halfway out of the water although Nelson had no idea what the tides were like here, so maybe they were lifted to their current location by higher water.

The submarine was lethal looking. The red bottom drew the eye, a visual insult to the white sand of the beach. A long sucker, probably fifty yards long at least. He didn't know the first thing about subs. It might be German, British, or American. Or Japanese for all he knew. It didn't have any markings except some sort of fish painted on the tower in the middle of the ship.

But it was missing a large part of the side. Nelson peered into the decking. Something had torn the ship open lengthwise and it didn't look like an explosion. The opening wasn't round enough. So probably not a torpedo or a mine. Streaks on the metal of the hull looked like claw marks, to his eyes.

The decks inside were mangled, as if something worked hard to get inside for some reason.

“What could do that to a metal ship?” Nelson asked.

“I don’t know,” McKinney said, “but the Brit ship is in the exact same shape except the other side is torn open.”

“You saw it?” Nelson asked.

McKinney nodded.

“There might be supplies we can use on those boats,” Nelson said, starting to stand up.

“You might want to rethink that,” McKinney said, grabbing Nelson’s sleeve and dragging him back down to the rock.

“Why?” Nelson asked, his tone suspicious. He didn’t need more trouble.

“Give it a few minutes. Watch the ship, not the sub.”

The ship was British for sure, it still had a remnant of the flag flying. The designator D-48 adorned the side. Most of the superstructure was forward leaving the back two-thirds of the deck flat for guns and other weapons.

A few quiet minutes passed, but finally the destroyer started shimmying. It rolled slightly on the bottom of the hull, then the sound of tearing metal reached his ears. Something big crawled out of the wreck.

A frog-bear-lizard.

For lack of a better descriptor.

It had four splayed legs, some areas of fur on its back, its head was wide but the face looked more like a bear, other than the huge mouth. The mouth looked like a 'gators, if Nelson had to choose, but it was shorter and wide. A reptilian tail stretched several yards behind it, vertical as if it was also designed to swim like a 'gator.

The body was round and seemingly engorged.

The beast dropped a sailor's body on the sand, then lunged back into the structure of the ship. The cove grew quiet once more.

Nelson's blood ran cold. This one creature, as far as he knew, was responsible for the death and destruction he saw below. It was harvesting the fruits of its foul work to feed, judging by the waste piles scattered around.

The presence of the beast explained why Nelson didn't see any shipping in the Channel. He'd hoped to signal a ship and make an escape from Brittany. But the only option now, if beasts like that patrolled the waters, was to leave by aircraft and hope a dragon didn't see them.

"Any of you boys know how to fly a plane?" Nelson asked.

Nobody answered.

"Great," he muttered. "Let's get back to town. We'll scavenge what we can, then we're headin' west toward the original US beachheads. Maybe someone's still alive back that way."

They climbed down to the safer cove, across to the French town, and searched for useful materials until dark. The next morning, they set out once more.

"Wonder why we're not seeing any dead trying to get to us?" Wilcox asked.

Nelson shook his head and kept putting one boot in front of the other as he walked away from the beauty of Étables-sur-Mer. "Shut up, Corporal."

"There's got to—"

"Wilcox, you say another word and I'll make you leave the squad."

Fifteen minutes of silence later they marched northwest on a two-lane road. A road sign said it was fifteen kilometers to Lanloup.

"We'll scavenge again there. That's our goal for today," Nelson told his men. "We'll probably be in Brest in a few days, hopefully our boys still hold it."

If, for any reason it wasn't safe toward the west, they were dead men walking.

Chapter 16 - Travel

The four crossbows Harry's squad owned were fantastic. The only problem was that the weapons shot the bolts too hard, and the ammo either sailed into the distance not to be found or embedded in a tree so deep it couldn't be recovered.

But it was a good thing they had the weapons. They shot much like a rifle, and because of that, they were able to learn to use them quickly. Otherwise they wouldn't eat meat. Watching the men use the longbows was like watching boys use a slingshot for the first time. Within three days they were out of arrows from practice. Any attempt at hunting with the longbow was guaranteed to fail, so they didn't even try.

He watched the last arrow sail over a tree and disappear into the blue of the sky.

"Parker, that's the worst shot I've seen yet," Harry chided.

"Give me a rifle any day," the infantryman grumbled back. "This is barbaric."

"You say that because you're the worst at using a bow. And not slightly worse. When you shoot, people behind you are terrified for the sake of their vital organs."

The other men laughed. At least their pauses to practice the weapons kept spirits up. Even Cylethe was amused. "If dek hunters shot bows like that, the tribe wouldn't eat."

"And if humans hadn't invented guns, a large number of the Undek would have been eaten," Miller said.

She glared coldly at her apprentice. "You have done the

exercises I gave you, Elementalist?"

"I have."

"Then you start the campfire for this night," she ordered him. "And if you fail, you will eat your rations raw."

Miller frowned but turned around to face the fire ring that several of the squad had just finished.

"Stack the wood," Harry ordered, eager to see where Miller was in his training.

The men quickly filled the ring with fresh cut deadfall. They were as eager for the fire as anyone else, as the last three days had seen a rise in altitude of at least a few thousand feet. Frost was on the ground that last morning as they woke up. The terrain, still wooded, thinned ahead further up the trail into the Aldikki mountain range. Each night would be colder, and each morning more miserable as they climbed. That difficulty would be multiplied by a dozen times once winter came on full bore. A miserable journey to reach them was part of the defense the Dek counted on.

"Light it," Cylethe demanded. "Use the words."

"*Sagunichallus nal victus segor*," Miller said in a language that sounded ancient. The radioman's hands, outstretched toward the waiting woodpile, twitched with nerves.

Smoke rolled from the cone created by Miller's fingers, rising quickly into the sky. Miller tore his palms apart and exclaimed his surprise.

"Wrong word," Cylethe said, laughing. "You summoned smoke, a combination of elemental air and elemental fire. Your words were 'summoning the offspring of minor fire'. You want the qualifier *vin*. You can make a great fire, but the test of control is to make a small one. Do it now."

Miller, to his credit, bowed to his teacher. Then took up his casting stance once again. "*Sagunichallus vin victus segor*," he growled out, and a small globe of fire appeared in the center of his outstretched fingers.

"*Sagunimallutik nal segroni*," he added to his chant. The bead of fire shot straight out from his hands, into the fire pit. The wood caught immediately from the intense heat of magical flame.

Harry wondered how it was that Miller didn't seem affected by the heat he summoned.

The men cheered and took out burning sticks to start two more fire pits with. Enough for everyone to have a warm seat.

"Well done, Miller!" Harry encouraged. "You're a right magician!"

"It's something I never imagined," Miller said. "I had no idea."

"You know a few tricks a child might know. Elementalists are rare," Cylethe said, "no matter what the race. Hagirr will want you so he can corrupt you to his side. It's up to this group to keep you from him."

"How do we do that?" Harry asked. "You say he's the most powerful wizard on this world."

"Everything has limits, Harry," Cylethe said. "I am limited, and so is Hagirr."

"Why?" Miller asked her. "How do you know what your limits are?"

"Each magician is a conduit. As your training starts, you will be limited by your ability to control magic. Later, your limitation will be how much magic you can focus and use from the universe around us. Think of yourself as a valve," Cylethe told him. "Every mage has a different limit as to how far the valve can open."

"That makes sense," Miller said. "I can feel the flow."

"I'm glad it makes sense to you," Parker quipped.

Harry frowned. "That's what's important. I don't see you starting any campfires in the chill, so I'm not too worked up about it not making sense to you." He turned to face the outspoken private. "In fact, Parker, after seeing you shoot today, you should probably learn at least one useful skill sometime soon, you lazy sot."

The rest of the men laughed.

"You laughing sorts think you're any better? We need to learn the skills our ancestors had a thousand years ago."

"You going to learn magic then, Lieutenant?" Parker shot back.

Harry laughed. The men weren't afraid to give it back to him. "It doesn't make any sense to me either." He touched his sword. "But guard duty does, and we all know how to do that. We'll do our standard roster, rotating one spot. Three on first are now on second, and so on. Third watch last night sleeps all night tonight."

Groans from a few of his soldiers.

“None of that, we have our duty. Except last night’s third… oh, is that me?” he asked, mockingly. “I should turn in then while you lads watch my back and listen to my snores.”

Ten minutes later exhaustion claimed him. Even leaders needed to refresh from time to time.

He dreamed of Miller erupting into a firestorm that swept all their enemies into ash.

* * *

The next days passed, and Harry’s team climbed ever higher. Crossing what had to be ten thousand meters above where they’d entered this world, the Aldikki peaks still towered much higher. Harry was always told that breathing at such an altitude was a task for only the most fit, but the air of Aerth seemed as abundant to him at their current height as it did when they spent the summer below.

Another bit of knowledge to add to his list of misunderstood things.

An airship approached the party from the west, rising along with the grade of the mountains. A dirigible, much like the Hindenburg had been, but this one looked more haphazard. A steam engine belched smoke into the sky, spinning a lazy blade that propelled the monstrosity.

“What in the name of the Father is that?” Jenkins asked.

Cylethe landed just ahead of the marching squad, in six inches of snow. She dismounted quickly, then ran to Harry. “Gnomes. Whether there is violence or not depends on what clan.”

“Should we hide?” Harry asked. “Prepare our guns?”

"You and I will stay here. The rest of your men should prepare as you did to kill the half-horses."

Harry ordered his men into positions. "Do not engage unless they engage us."

Cylethe sent the *drakon* into the air, ready to attack if the need should arise.

The dirigible climbed until level with the Brits and Cylethe, then rose straight up while drifting slightly up the trail. A rope ladder dropped over the side and fell precisely onto the trail. They had a skilled pilot.

A head popped over the railing that ran along the side of the dirigible's undercarriage. Cylethe grabbed Harry's hand and wrapped it around the amulet she wore.

"Oy!" the head called down to them. "We seek to trade. Come on board if you like."

"What clan are you?" Cylethe asked.

"Flitterboots," the creature replied, confusing Harry. Had the amulet not worked?

"The runners from troubles?" Cylethe yelled up.

"That is a nasty rumor," the creature answered. "We never run. We fly."

Cylethe grinned at Harry. "It's safe. You can call your men down to us."

A few minutes later the group was one again. As that happened, one of the beings climbed down the ladder, which Harry noticed had extremely close rungs. Now Harry understood why. The spokesmen of the Flitterboots was no more than three feet tall if an inch.

"I'm Sorbiloonisorb," the gnome said. "I can invite two of you to the deck to discuss trade if you like, if you have anything of value."

Harry noticed that Sorbi-whatever didn't actually touch the ground. He stayed on the ladder, interlocking his arms through the rungs to help hold his weight. A small crossbow hung on his back, but it was hard to imagine the little guy getting angry. "You and I," he said to Cylethe. "No more than two of us can understand them anyway. But what would they want that we might have? And what might they have for us?"

"They'll pay a lot for something they haven't seen before," she answered. "And you have quite a few things they haven't seen before if you're willing to part with such treasures."

"I'll gather some things from the men."

"Sorbiloonisorb, we would be most honored to trade with the Flitterboots," Cylethe said to the gnome as Harry called his men in for a huddle. He didn't understand the response; he was no longer touching the amulet. But it sounded very sing-songy.

"Men, I need trade items to swap with these fellows. They seem friendly enough, and we might get some things we can use."

"I've got my lighter," Wilkes offered. "I'm out of smokes anyway."

Three more men offered lighters.

"Flint and steel?" Parker offered.

"They'll have that," Harry said. "Besides, what if Miller gives out on us? We'll need something to light fires."

Lars tossed a flask onto the growing collection on the ground. "Ah hae some cratur in that."

"Scotch?" Harry asked. "You'd part with that?"

"Weel it doesn't keek lik' ah will be getting ony mair, wull ah?" the Scotsman said, indignant. "A dram is worth a lot, bit living thro' this is something tae."

"We're all going to live through it," Harry said, shaking his head. "I appreciate the sacrifice. Anything else?"

"We got our gas masks," Garrett replied. "We're not using those."

Harry started to agree, but then he remembered the weapon Cylethe's *drakon* used on the half-horses. "No, we keep those." He sighed. "Three lighters and a flask of scotch."

Miller handed over a pocketknife. A fine specimen with several blades.

"You sure?" Harry asked.

A nod and a weak smile was his only answer. Harry thought he remembered Miller saying something about the knife being a gift from his father.

He grabbed the small pile and headed to the ladder. Sorbiwhats was already back on deck, and Cylethe was climbing. The *drakon* complained from somewhere overhead, but she kept going. So Harry climbed too.

The deck wasn't far from the balloons of whatever it was that made the dirigible float. Four feet at most, but then the occupants of the craft weren't tall enough for that to matter to them. A small horde of them gathered around as Cylethe and Harry sat cross legged on the deck. She held out the amulet for him to once again clasp onto.

"Can we get you anything as a refreshment?" Sorbitoots asked. "Wine? Ale?"

A cold wind blew across the deck, then one of the gnomes turned some valves on pipes that ran underneath the balloon. Soon warm air radiated downward toward the deck.

"Ale," Cylethe answered. "For both myself and my human."

Her human?

He let it go for now, filing a note to ask later. "Yes, ale."

After some introductions and the serving of refreshments, the gnomes got straight to business.

"What have you got to trade?" Sorbsnots asked.

"We have some trinkets, the likes of which I suspect you haven't seen," Cylethe stated. "The first are three lighting boxes."

Harry lit a lighter then flipped the lid back down on it. He opened it and it was out. He lit it again. Then repeated the process again.

"Is that magic or machine?" Sorbonobs asked, clearly interested.

"Machine," Harry replied. "It runs off very refined pitch."

"Excellent," the gnome exclaimed. "We can make just such a fuel."

"What else do you have?"

"We have a liquor from Earth, probably the only example of which exists on Aerth," Cylethe said. "It's in a finely crafted metal flask, which could itself be used for a potion or the like after the liquor is consumed."

"I'd like to taste it," Sorbinoodles said.

"Not going to happen," Cylethe said. "There are only a few mouthfuls, which is, as I said, all that exists that you might find. You may, however, smell it."

Harry opened the flask and waved it under Sorboneedles substantial nose.

"It smells delicious," the gnome smiled. "What else?"

Harry opened the blades of the pocketknife. The gnomes on the deck jostled one another for a closer look. Clearly, they liked the tool.

"What is that you carry?" Sorbisuits asked Harry, pointing at the sidearm in his holster.

"My defense weapon," Harry replied. "A gun."

"How does that work? Would you trade it?"

"The price would be very high," Harry said, reluctantly. He didn't want to, but everything had a price.

Sorbisnooker opened his arms up wide. “We will begin making offers for the items, and if we can agree, we will trade.” The other gnomes nodded their agreement. “We will discuss among ourselves below deck and return in a moment.”

Only seconds passed before Cylethe and Harry sat alone on the deck. The sound of things being tossed around echoed up through the wood under them. The only other sound was faint wind noises through the ropes of the dirigible and the whoosh of the large propeller that kept the airship in position.

“We sure could get to the winter grounds faster with one of these,” Harry commented.

“Don’t even joke about it. These airships are like temples to the gnomes. You’d basically be asking them to sell out their gods.”

“Got it. The airship is out of bounds.”

“Besides, you’re not rich enough by orders of magnitude.”

He sighed. “The story of my life.”

The gnomes returned and began piling items on the deck. Flasks, sacks, foodstuffs, what looked like gemstones. Something interesting caught Harry’s eye. Weapons that he assumed were dwarven in make based upon the crossbows his squad already had.

He wanted those.

A fact that wasn’t lost on Sorbispittle. “You appreciate Dwarven artisanship?”

“I do,” Harry replied. “I would trade for those first.”

“Two crossbows for the lot,” the gnome replied immediately.

Cylethe coughed loudly. “Are you mad?”

“Every negotiation starts somewhere.”

“It shouldn’t start with an insult to our intelligence,” she retorted, a bit of anger in her voice.

“What do you consider to be fair, magician?”

“All the crossbows and swords for the three lighters. With ammunition for the bows.”

“That’s thirty bows then?” the gnome sputtered. “And a like number of swords?”

“Indeed,” she replied.

“Madness!” he spat out. “I wouldn’t pay half that number!”

“What number would you pay?” Harry asked, still very much interested.

“Ten of each, only because we want to see how the light boxes work and you have three of them.”

“Twelve,” Harry replied. “Of each. Plus, all the bolts you have for them.”

“Ten, and I’ll throw in a week’s fine rations for all of your humans,” Sorbisorts said to Cylethe. “Or, if you give us our own human, we’ll give you all the weapons.”

Cylethe looked at Harry.

“No,” Harry snapped.

She shrugged then turned back to the trader. "Ten bows, ten swords, we pick. Two hundred bolts. A week of fine rations. A keg of ale."

"Deal!" he shouted, louder than Harry would have expected he could. The other gnomes on deck broke out in dance and song. The dancing took nearly two minutes while he stared on incredulously. They certainly were a happy people.

Once the dance was over the trading continued.

"We might as well see what you want for the liquor," Sorbisinger said. "I wouldn't wish to insult such a great magician again. I prefer not to be a toad."

The gnomes laughed.

"Healing brew," Cylethe said. "Twenty flasks."

"A fortunate thing we have some straight from the Shingar Seacoast," Sorbisloop replied. "I agree."

During the song and dance that followed, Cylethe's expression fell. "I should have asked for more," she whispered to Harry.

Once the songs died away, trade for the last item began. "And the knife of many knives?" the gnome asked. "What for that?"

"What do we need?" Harry asked Cylethe.

"I feel you bested me on the last trade," Cylethe said. "You make an offer, Sorbiloonisorb."

Harry was relieved to hear the name again. Too bad he still didn't quite understand it.

Sorbilooniesnorts smiled. "I will offer a set of Dek leather that keeps the wearer comfortable in any temperature."

Cylethe nodded. "We'll make that deal."

The deck of the airship erupted in song and dance once again. Two gnomes ran below and appeared a short time later with a set of leather armor much like he'd seen Undek warriors wear on patrol.

"And for the… gun you called it?" the trader said, surprising Harry.

He stared at the gnome a minute, who stared back, grinning.

"Could you show me how it works?" the trader asked.

"That is in itself, valuable," Cylethe said. "Are you willing to pay to see?"

The gnome slid a gem over to Harry. "I am."

Harry had no idea what the gem was, or what it was worth. But Cylethe seemed pleased and the deal was already made.

He explained the gun and the workings of it to Sorbiloonibin, including the safe handling procedures.

"I'd like to have that one to develop more from," the gnome said, when the demonstration was over. "A weapon like that would command value with the elves and dwarves."

"I am not sure—"

"— if you want to trade away such an advantage?" the trader asked. "Of course you don't. But what if I gave you something of equal advantage that is much harder for me to duplicate, but much more useful to you?" He clapped his hands gleefully. "After all, I only see six of those— cartridges you called them? Your weapon only works six times unless you can get more of the cartridges, yes?"

Harry sighed. It was entirely too painfully true.

"I thought so," the trader laughed. "I have a trade I think we'll both like." He turned to a gnome nearby, one with baubles all over his leather jacket. "Run and get me *Dynamus*, Elomostookkimarilom."

The decorated gnome ran off, returning a short time later with a sword in a scabbard. The weapon was human, elven or dek sized. "I obtained this off a trader over twenty years ago. He had a bit of a gambling problem and this settled that debt."

The trader placed the sword gently on the deck in front of Harry. "It was a substantial debt."

Harry picked up the scabbard, and he would swear on a Bible the sword hummed inside. Almost as if it were purring.

The hilt of the sword was wrapped in maroon leather, and a stone lay in the pommel. A clear stone, with a blue energy dancing inside.

"What is it?" Harry asked, awestruck.

"It likes you," Sorbiloonsnips said. "It is an intelligent creation from long ago. Few have the knowledge to make such a wonder now, but here is your chance to own one."

Harry looked at Cylethe. It was almost as if the sword was calling to him. "Is this real?"

She chanted off a spell and the swords hilt glowed with a bright purple aura. “Very much so. This is a trade that I would take, Harry. I believe you’ve reached a point in your life where destiny is determined by the choice you make.”

“And the destiny of our clan,” the trader said. “Everyone wins, human.”

Harry handed the pistol and some ammunition to Sorbiloonisorb. Suddenly the gnome’s name seemed very clear.

“I accept.”

“Don’t you wish to test it first?” the gnome asked. “See how it feels?”

“I think, sir, you know I don’t have to do that.”

The gnome smiled. Of course he knew. “It is a weapon that seemed more suited for you, otherwise I’d never have parted with it. Now that you have it, the universe seems to be more correct.”

He didn’t yet know why, but Harry knew that was true. Reality was a better place with the sword in his hands.

Chapter 17 - The Underways

Irsu had traveled the Underways, also called the Deepways or the Underroads, as a younger dwarf. He'd worked as a laborer for cargo caravans. He knew what they were in for during their trip to a distant hold.

"You're thinking," Coragg commented.

"We're in a bad way," Irsu replied, where the guards could hear him as well. "We don't have a trade banner. We don't have a priest of any kind. It's unlikely that any hold is going to open their gates to us. They might even attack us as brigands."

"What do we do?" Coragg asked.

"Excursion," Irsu replied.

Coragg groaned. "We're not scouts!"

"I am," Numo said. "I've been on more excursions than you've had ladies."

"So more than one then?" Irsu quipped.

The guards laughed as Coragg scowled.

"And you, the lot of you. You're clearly no longer royal guards," Irsu added. "You're members of the Iron now, Iron platoon, Iron company, from Iron Mountain Hold. Your allegiance is to our survival, not any nonsense, you got it?"

Mumbles of agreement, reluctant sounding, but Irsu could sense that they were relieved he'd given them status. As the *Amblu-gane*, he could conscript soldiers. While these were already his by word of the Underking, they were now officially his by the authority he possessed.

"We're going to find a way out. Numo is an amazing scout, he's been my trusted eyes for a few years now. I have no doubts to our success."

Livelier responses greeted those words. He was appearing as if he had a plan. Something they needed to see, no matter how marginally true it was. The plan consisted of simply finding a natural path to the surface. Once there they'd find a way to the Hagirr gate and back to Earth.

Hevreg be damned. Even if she did have the pale dwarf sickness, something was bothering Irsu about what happened in the Royal Quarter. Hers was the only irrational voice in the old Iron Mountain Hold. Why was she so affected with madness while the guards were fine?

"We're away from the eyes of our clan and we have a long journey," Coragg said. "We should rest and prepare for a solid march tomorrow. Hopefully these lizards will fit where we need to go, otherwise packs will get heavier."

No complaints. That was good. The soldiers listened as Coragg gave them the watch rotation, leaving Irsu out.

"I take watch as well," he said. "I'll rotate with Degrin and Mikun."

Coragg nodded. His expression showed he'd hoped Irsu would do as much. "Four watches, three dwarves each. You will watch with the same team every night. I'll assign the portion of your watch based upon your performance that day. If everyone is at peak, then we'll rotate one slot." He pointed at Irsu and his two watchmates. “You’re first. Wake me in two hours.”

Irsu chuckled. His second was clearly eager to get to bed barking out orders like that. “Two hours,” he agreed, trusting his innate sense of time to get it right. Living underground, separated from the sun, an internal clock was essential.

Nights passed uneventfully as did days for some time. The underways, always a challenge, were kind to them. They made as little noise as plate armored dwarves could, but if there was trouble nearby, it would find them.

They came to a bridge across a chasm. Below them water rushed, invisible in the depths below. The far side of the bridge was too distant to see.

The bridge, built by dwarves that lived long before Irsu was born, was suspended from thick cables sunk into the walls that rose into the darkness above. He’d been on two or three caravans that came this way before. The bridge would support no more than one wagon at a time as the merchants crossed.

It would easily support Irsu’s squad, even with the two pack lizards.

“We cross together,” he ordered. “If you’re afraid of heights, don’t look over the side.”

His soldiers scoffed at the idea they’d be afraid. But he’d make mental note which ones didn’t stray too near the edge. It was his duty to know the strengths of these warriors. As they wouldn’t confess to any weakness, it was his to find it himself.

“Numo, do you know where the river we hear goes?” Coragg asked.

"Deeper, to a sea I've never seen. So the words I've been told said."

They didn't need to go deeper. That wasn't the way.

As they neared the other side, a sight they didn't expect waited for them. About forty dwarves, all with pale skin and dead looking eyes. White hair jetted out from under black tinted helms. Most of the dwarves wore leather, but a dozen or so wore chain or platemail.

Twenty of the dwarves raised crossbows. There was no mistaking their intent.

One of the three that wore platemail beckoned to them, summoning them forward. Undoubtedly the leaders, the one that gestured wore a black cape that partially wrapped around to the front. For the first time that Irsu knew of, a symbol was associated with the pale dwarves.

An eight-pointed starburst. A very strange symbol indeed for a subterranean people.

"Shields," Coragg cried.

Thankfully the royal guardsmen were some of the best trained warriors in Iron Mountain clan, which helped make up for the fact they'd rarely, if ever, seen combat. The soldiers immediately formed a two-high layered wall of shields. Hidden behind steel, Irsu listened as bolts exploded into fragments against the barrier. He thanked Ekesstu that these troops also carried excellent equipment.

"What's the plan?" Coragg said, looking at him. "We can retreat backwards, but then we're trapped in the underway to Iron Mountain Hold with no other exit. We'll be driven all the way back to locked gates."

"Good assessment," Irsu agreed. He peeked around the end of the shield wall to see the enemy. The bows were reloading. The enemy looked well stocked. There was no going ahead or back.

He looked over the side. "Light a torch," he commanded Numo.

Torch lit, he took it from Numo and threw it over the side. It fell a few dozen *kadros* to the river below. The water revealed some secrets before it killed the fire. The river was shallow, with many rocks that made the noise they heard from the bridge. It covered the bottom fully, but a dwarf with a pack lizard could travel such a terrain.

"Samek, Horgra... lower your shields and get your crossbows from the front lizard," Irsu ordered. "I will do the same. We're going to deter them from following us back across the bridge long enough for me to make the plan I have work. Coragg and Numo, you'll handle the lizards." He pointed at the bolts sticking from the packed supplies on top of the front lizard. "Keep them behind the shield wall best you can."

The soldiers did as ordered.

"Defensive retreat," Coragg ordered once he and Numo had the animals under control.

The party backed slowly away from the enemy as another wave of bolts struck the shield wall. Soon they'd be out of sight of the enemy, and then the sickly dwarves would probably move onto the bridge.

"Stand ready," Irsu ordered the other two archers. "After the next wave of bolts, we'll fire straight down the line of the bridge."

A minute later bolts clacked against steel once more. The crossbow wielding dwarves stepped from cover, aimed as best they could, and fired.

A couple of screams met their efforts, one of which changed in pitch and fell away into the void below. The archers retreated again to cover.

Irsu wished he could still see the enemy, but he at least knew the path they had to take to approach. He could hold the far side of the bridge indefinitely.

Until they starved.

He waited to see if another bolt barrage would come, but it didn't. The enemy was probably considering their options. The three archers reloaded and fired again. No screams. Either the enemy had a shield wall up as well, or they'd left the bridge.

Both situations suited his need.

"Coragg, you're not going to like this next bit. Everyone is to tie themselves off to the pack lizards."

Coragg stared at him a moment. "Have the lizards climb down the wall? You've gone mad."

"Do it," he ordered. "However many the animal can hold, you think. Then shuttle those to the river below and come back for more."

"You don't think like a person should," Coragg complained as he did as ordered. Three of the shields disappeared as Coragg tied them to the pack and himself to the saddle seat on the front of the pack. “Into the abyss,” he said as the lizard disappeared over the side.

Irsu and the other archers fired again. A horde of bolts fired back, one of which struck Horgra in the shoulder. The well-trained dwarf didn’t utter a sound as he spun around and fell.

“Keep firing,” Irsu said to Samek. “And pick up the rate if you can.”

He went to look at Horgra’s wound. He dragged the warrior behind the shield wall and examined what happened. The bolt passed clean through the front layer of armor, through Horgra’s upper chest, possibly hitting a lung. The bolt passed partway out the back plate, but stopped there. When Horgra fell he’d landed on the bolt, breaking it off and twisting the rest inside.

Irsu marveled that the warrior had fallen silently.

“We’re taking you down next.” Irsu lifted Horgra’s head into his lap. “We’ll tend the wound at the bottom in the ravine.”

“Nay,” Horgra said. “Spin me ‘round, give me my bow, and I’ll hold them while you and the others escape. We have no priest and you and I both know this is a mortal wound.”

Irsu hadn’t known that for sure, but the blood that trickled from Horgra’s mouth confirmed it probably was.

“I’m sorry,” Irsu said. “I planned on getting us all out.”

“I will die fighting,” Horgra said. “How often does a King’s Guard get to say that?”

Irsu smiled. “Not often, I expect.”

“Set me up. I’ll fight. Ekesstu and Mordain will fight over my essence in the afterlife.”

“I’ve no doubt,” Irsu said as he arranged Horgra facing the right way and gave him his crossbow.

“Take my sword to my mother,” Horgra said. “I won’t be needing it.”

“I will,” Irsu promised.

Coragg touched Irsu on the arm. “It’s time for the next lot. That will leave you,” he looked down at Horgra, “this warrior and Samek to hold them off. You go down. I’ll stand with Samek.”

“No,” Irsu said, a bit indignant. “You come back for us. Horgra will be staying to guard our retreat.”

Coragg nodded and began tying off the next batch of shield bearers. Samek and Irsu leaned a shield in front of them, giving themselves cover as the next flurry of bolts struck.

Irsu looked down at Horgra. The dwarf was dead. He reached out from cover to close the hero’s eyes. This was Hevreg’s fault. Her madness was costing lives. When Irsu reached King Scorriss once more, he’d demand justice.

“It’s just you and me now, Samek,” Irsu said.

“Aye,” Samek replied. He pointed at Horgra. “If they hadn’t killed him, we’d have just enough to storm across and teach those oafs a lesson.”

Irsu smiled at the bravado. “I hope we’ve sent a dozen of

them into the next world. Horgra deserves a price to be paid."

"We'll have to assume we have," Samek agreed. "We are, after all, of the Iron."

"A reasonable assumption then," Irsu said as he shot another bolt into the darkness. "But I still hope Coragg hurries."

"The lizards can scale walls only so fast," Samek said. "My father raised them when I was young, before the last holdwar."

"We'll be fine," Irsu said to reassure both of them. "Keep firing."

After what seemed like an eternity, Coragg appeared on the wall to the right of the bridge, strapped into the pack saddle of his lizard. He tossed two looped ropes to the archers. "Best I can do for you, since we're not going to have any cover."

Irsu grabbed the nearest rope and moved to the edge of the precipice. He stuck a foot in the loop then stepped off. The rope jerked as he fell a short distance and swung, he hoped the sticky feet of the lizard held. He felt another jerk as Samek did the same, then swung into him.

"Horgra?" Coragg yelled.

"Dead," Irsu shouted back up to his friend. "Let's go."

The lizard skittered down the wall, slower than ever due to the strange weight of two dwarves hanging below him. The lizard's face leered above Irsu, making him glad the beast ate fungi as a regular diet. Otherwise he and Samek might seem like dangling treats.

After a small eternity they reached the floor of the ravine, the bridge lost in the darkness above.

"Numo, you've scouted?" Irsu asked.

"I have. Upriver is no path at all. The ravine closes up, turning the river on its side. There the water rages, narrow and deep. We would never pass."

"Deeper we go then," Irsu said. "Eventually we'll find our way up."

The dwarves regrouped and began their trek down river. Irsu looked at the faces of the soldiers. Grim, but spirited. Each wanted to make Horgra's life-price worth paying, he was certain.

The darkness summoned them deeper, and as it did it drew Irsu's thoughts deeper as well.

The sickly dwarves hadn't tried to negotiate. They hadn't called out or made any symbols of peace. They'd tried to capture Irsu's team, then attacked when the Iron Mountain clan warriors refused to surrender, killing Horgra.

If Irsu saw them again, a life-price would certainly be paid.

Chapter 18 - Jangik

July 18, 1940

The gates of Jangik lay open as Ernst's entourage approached. Formidable walls surrounded the city, twenty meters high and at least ten meters thick. The outside surface of the walls seemed unscarred by any war. What they were built to keep out was an unknown.

The procession rode to the foot of a palace complex the likes of which Ernst had never seen. One a bit like what he imagined Rome's palaces to have been during the rule of the Emperors. Powerful men often built monuments to vanity.

Broad marble steps rose to golden doors as the party stopped, but of more interest was the group awaiting them at the bottom of those steps.

Another twenty or so elves, much like Elianna.

And a human. A young male, half Ernst's age, the man looked about twenty. His clothing, however, indicated some grand rank within the city, possibly even the man Elianna said she served.

Elianna leapt from her horse and landed on the ground with the grace and dignity of any acrobat. She didn't run, but she took long strides as she approached the human, then embraced him with vigor. They kissed for over a minute while the Germans grew uncomfortable.

They finally separated, and Elianna gestured toward the riders.

"Lord Hagirr, may I present Director Ernst Haufmann and his wife, the Lady Herta Haufmann. They are emissaries from Germany, a nation of Earth."

Ernst dismounted and immediately bowed his head.

"Ernst, this is Hagirr, the greatest wizard and ruler of Aerth."

"The entire world?" Herta asked, incredulous. "Or is that a false claim like so many rulers on Earth engage in?"

Ernst flinched, but Elianna laughed. "Yes, Herta, the entire world." She turned to her lover. "Earth is a mess of fractured nation states. Germany is trying to correct this."

If the wizard was offended, he gave no indication. He simply smiled at Herta as if Ernst's wife were simple. "Let us discuss such matters over dinner. What shall I call you?" he asked, looking at Ernst, then smiling at Herta.

"My name is Ernst, Lord. Ernst will do fine for me, and Herta for my wife."

"Then I am Hagirr," Hagirr replied, smiling at Herta and bowing slightly. "Hagirr will do fine for me."

Ernst wondered if the man was taunting him, but then the wizard laughed.

"Come. We will celebrate in my palace."

Elianna barked orders to the guards around her and Ernst and Herta's travel bags were grabbed, then carried up toward the palace.

Ernst looked at the front of the building. What wonders awaited inside such a wondrous structure in a world of magic?

Seated in a great hall only half an hour later, he got an

answer to his question. A monstrously long table sat in the center line of the room. He and Herta were seated as guests of honor to the left of Hagirr's end seat, and Elianna and Trisari sat across from them. Elianna's family lined the table down her side, Ernst's pilots and guards lined his.

Beings the likes of which he never imagined served dinner and entertained. On a stage at one end of the hall a dozen gossamer thin beings with the voices of angels sang softly, the perfect acoustics of the room carried the harmonies and melodies to the ears of every occupant. Art that maintained greater detail the closer you got to it for examination decorated gold encrusted walls. A being that seemed to be mostly plant grew a fruit unknown to Ernst on an extended arm and dropped it on Ernst's plate, only to do the same a moment later for Herta and then so on down the table.

A hundred diners sat in chairs arranged neatly in a row, and Ernst noticed a curious phenomenon. When he looked at any one of the diners, or if they addressed him, he would hear them with perfect clarity.

Crystal plates sat on silk tablecloths. The same crystals decorated chandeliers that glowed with neither electricity nor fire. At the fast end of the table a giant chair housed a creature that was twenty feet tall when it stood up, looking every bit like a human with a distorted body.

"A giant," Elianna told him. "Aerth clan. The Storm clan is much, much larger."

Ernst had no idea how it even got into the room.

Females of various races danced nude around the table, their bodies perfect in every way, their synchronous movements unnaturally timed. Every perfect dancer turned and ran into a central dancer, to become one. She bowed and the hall applauded her performance.

Hagirr tapped a goblet, and the ring of the cup silenced everyone at the table. "We welcome our first guests from the nation of Germany, these representatives of Earth, Ernst and Herta Haufmann." He raised the goblet. "Tonight, we show them the grandeur of Aerth. We will dine, then, if time permits, I will show them the Great White Pyramid of Jangik." He laughed, and the attendees laughed along with him. "They've clearly been impressed by the palace. Wait until they climb the steps to the gods and see the gateway to the heavens!"

The noise in the hall quadrupled, and food service increased. Platters were presented loaded with meat, little of which Ernst recognized. He took some of everything. The liquor, ale, beer, whatever was in his own goblet was the best thing he'd ever consumed in his life. Copious fruits and vegetables entered his stomach well past when he should have stopped eating, yet he didn't feel full. The fruit dropped by the plant creature sprouted a face and looked at Ernst plaintively.

He turned it to face Elianna, who slammed her knife into it, cutting it in half. "You have to eat it in a timely fashion, Ernst, or it will mature and escape. The *escupa* breed like rabbits. We can't allow that."

Almost as if to verify Elianna's words, Herta shrieked, in shock more than fear. The thing on Herta's plate jumped up and ran toward the far end of the table, dodging back and forth between dishes and candelabras as if playing rugby. The diners stabbed at it with their forks and knives, but it deftly dodged them all.

"*Sagunimallutik nal Ingustivari*," Hagirr said.

The creature had almost made it to the far end, past the giant, when an invisible hand grabbed it and jerked it the thirty meters across the length of the table.

It landed in Hagirr's hands, and he took a bite as the thing squealed in protest.

"It's fine," the wizard said to Herta, smiling. "They taste far better if you wait until they can run." He extended his hand, the creature's fibrous legs now dangling lifelessly, offering it to Herta for her consumption.

Herta fainted onto Ernst's shoulder as Hagirr burst into laughter.

"Too much for her to take inside of one day?" the wizard asked. "We can visit the pyramid tomorrow. There is no need to stress your wife further." He leaned in toward Ernst. "Because if she's fainting at this, she should bring extra clothes with her for that excursion. She might soil herself. You haven't seen a thing yet."

Ernst wondered if that was a reference to the humiliation the dragon had heaped upon him, but said nothing.

After dinner servants showed Ernst and Herta to their rooms, where they discussed their predicament.

"There is something not right," Herta told Ernst.

"We should speak in private," Ernst responded, waving his hands toward the servants. "Ears abound."

Herta giggled. "They don't speak German! I'm just saying the man who hosted us for dinner… he doesn't seem as if he has a soul to me. It's as if he is the world to himself and the rest of us are unliving playthings."

"I noticed it too," Ernst agreed. "It's in his eyes. While his face is expressive, his eyes… they are devoid of presence."

"Unlike your elf?" Herta asked.

"She is cruel, but she knows others are beings too. She just rarely cares from what I see."

"Hmmmph."

Ernst sensed his wife didn't want him defending Elianna. He spoke no more of it, and neither did she, the awkwardness was short due to them arriving at their room. The grandeur of it swept Herta's displeasure with him away.

They climbed into bed on the most comfortable mattress he'd ever slept on in his life. Down filled blankets covered them, but despite that he slept next to a shivering wife.

He couldn't help but wonder if he was being brave enough for her. Because he wanted nothing more than to break down in fear himself. It was a day of macabre comedy. Tomorrow, it seemed, would be something else entirely.

Chapter 19 - A Narrow Way

July 19, 1940

A day after leaving Étables-sur-Mer, Nelson and his remaining men stumbled on a rear supply depot. Mostly untouched except for a few animal scavengers, the camp looked like the inhabitants had simply got up and left. In the mess tent food rotted on plates and on the serving line. A few forks lay on the ground, but most were on the table where diners had dropped them or set them down.

One crow, head cocked to the side, gave them the evil eye while holding a half-rotten strip of bacon in its mouth.

"This is the creepiest thing I've ever seen," Wilcox said, as he shooed off the bird. "Nature's taking what men left behind."

"You ain't lyin'" Nelson whispered. "Keep your voice down."

Nelson's squad consisted of another sergeant, William Gunter. Like the now dead Lieutenant Eads, he deferred to Nelson for some reason. He had Corporal Wilcox and Private McKinney from his original squad, as well as Private Connors. And, of course, Billy.

"I'm going to write down our names and post them up in the command tent," Nelson said, "in case anyone does come this way and attempt a rescue. They'll know we're on our way to Brest. You guys stick together, look for non-perishable food and any weapons we might want to take along." He sniffed. "And change your danged clothes. You all stink."

"Should we get a vehicle?" Connors asked.

Nelson shook his head. "It'd be nice, but we'd just draw attention to ourselves. We travel on foot and quietly as we have been. No deader's got us yet." He thought a minute. "But if you see a radio, I'd like to know about that."

They split up and he went to the command tent, which was easy to find. It wasn't a big camp, and what there was had consisted more of supplies than men apparently.

He opened the front flap and walked in, his Colt in his hand. He left the flap open to let light into the tent.

Not a single soul inside. He sat down at what was probably the commanding officer's desk. Lieutenant Colonel Alfred Manning, the paperwork sitting around the desk read.

A cigar sat cold in an ashtray on the desk. Nelson picked it up and shoved it in his mouth to chew on. He'd lost his last one at the mess hall a few days ago during the attack on the line.

Nothing in the front part of the tent indicated what happened to the men.

A canvas wall separated the front from the back half. He opened the wooden door built into the wall and a smell hit him immediately. Someone was dead inside.

"Lord, don't let this be a deader," he whispered, gripping his Colt tighter and stepping inside the much darker area.

He stepped in something sticky. Nothing moved to attack him, but he did make out a dark mass on the floor. Certain that it wouldn't be seen in the distance through the canvas of the tent, he pulled his flashlight from his belt. He sighed deeply as he turned it on, tired of horror, tired of death.

A circle of light told him everything he needed to know.

A body on the floor lay crumpled in the fetal position. The clothes were shredded, but he made out the silver rank of a Lieutenant Colonel. This was the commander. Why was his the only body in camp?

A pistol lay on the floor, spent casings were scattered about. The commander hadn't gone down without a struggle.

The stickiness that Nelson was stepping in was the colonel's blood. The body itself looked like something had dissolved the flesh where the clothing was ripped.

He didn't need to see any more. He holstered his own pistol.

Deaders had been here but looked to be gone now. Either the men of the camp had run away, or they were led off in the deader trap the Army had warned Nelson about.

His band of refugees would need to be doubly careful. If the deaders were here in force to take even this small camp, then Nelson's band would be no match at all.

He scanned the room. Office supplies and filing cabinets. Also, a hand cranked radio. That's what the colonel had died for, he was trying to get a message out. A warning, a call for help… Nelson had no way to know if the man was successful.

He grabbed the radio and laboriously hauled the behemoth device out of the tent and back to the mess hall.

The men were coming down the main street to join him, carrying what looked like quite a few supplies. And a wheelbarrow.

The radio was heavy, not exactly meant to be portable as it was full of vacuum tubes and a strong frame to mount the parts on. It looked like surplus equipment from the last war, to be honest. Despite the weight, he sat it up on one of the tables. He started cranking, wondering how much he had to work to get power. The dials on front lit up, the radio switch was on.

"*— BBC reporting —*" came from the speaker.

Hearing that, the men dropped their supplies at the door and rushed in, all of them talking at once.

"Can you get that back?" Gunter asked.

"Crank the handle," Nelson ordered Billy. The big kid jumped right on it.

"*— losses to aviation have been high, but Churchill assures the BBC that factories are ramping up production. He says that the dragons, although terrifying and difficult to kill, are vulnerable as the RAF has proved. The Prime Minister says that with enough brave men and stout aircraft the horde of evil creatures will be beaten back to wherever it is they come from.*"

"We can beat them," Wilcox said, grinning. "I want to live to see that."

"We all want to live," Nelson replied. "Ain't a one of us going to die if I can help it." He looked at the pile by the door. "Let's divvy up those supplies and figure out if we can take this radio along."

"It's huge," McKinney complained. "We only found one wheelbarrow."

"Do you want to know what's going on in the world?" Nelson asked. "We're taking it."

"I second that," Sergeant Gunter replied, backing Nelson up.

"This ain't a democracy," Nelson said, nodding at Gunter, "but I appreciate us being on the same page."

The men passed out ammunition, new rifles, pistols, and C-rations. The wheelbarrow was loaded up with the radio, a small tent, and more food.

"We're good for at least a week," McKinney said. "No need to go into the towns."

Nelson nodded. He wasn't sure why, but most of the towns felt like a trap to him. The US Army had spared most of the French villages from burning, choosing instead to clear them out with street fighting. A few of the larger towns weren't so lucky, those were now in smoking ruin since it was deemed too costly in men to take them.

Now the villages seemed like a place where death waited, their graveyards ready to create armies of deaders for whatever evil Satan had unleashed on the world.

"Just as planned," Wilcox said. "We need to get to Brest. These supplies should get us there and back here again if need be. We'll even have a bit of cushion if we move quickly."

"But only if we get moving," Nelson replied. "Let's go."

Chapter 20 – *Dynamus*

They'd left the Flitterboot gnomes two days earlier, and Harry couldn't help but feel he'd made new allies in this hostile world. But the most important part of the interchange rested on his back.

The sword *Dynamus*.

It was everything the gnome traders had promised. An intelligent weapon that conveyed to the wielder certain benefits. Harry wondered if there was also a price.

He now wore the armor from the trade. It fit perfectly. There was no cold for him. Despite the men around him complaining about the wind, Harry felt as if he were riding during a comfortable spring day. Harry's horse seemed to feel the same, so the armor must affect rider and beast.

The sword didn't talk to him so much as feel at him. Harry knew certain things about the weapon based upon those feelings. The sword was feeling triumphant now that it had found its way into the hands of a human again, and it gave him a sense of the nearly immeasurable time that had passed since the last human hands grasped it. The blade was human forged, and it seemed it was loyal to humanity.

Whenever Harry thought of their mission, to get back to Earth, or to find Hagirr and make him send Harry's men home, the sword was angry. Harry didn't know if it hated the idea of humans leaving Aerth, or if it hated Hagirr. It got equally upset when he thought of either concept.

So he thought of the matters at hand instead.

Hunting was now supplementing their stores. Cylethe mocked the British infantry for what bad hunters they were, but Harry thought them adequate. The dwarven crossbows and bolts made the job much easier. If Harry'd not seen the effect of the Elven bows they'd secured in France when used by a skilled archer, he'd think the thin and fragile-looking bows garbage.

The other men ignored the elven weapons now. Harry practiced with the slender bows every evening, however, with arrows he'd found in the dwarven supplies. Apparently, the gnomes had simply thrown the elven missiles into the pile, thinking them usable by the crossbows. The strength and grace of the weapons was an acquired taste, and as he practiced, Harry grew more fond of them.

He was getting better, and he was attempting to make his own arrows. At that he was not getting much better, but his efforts were entertaining Cylethe.

Stopping for the day, they set up camp in the way that had become the norm. Tents facing the fire in a circle. Miller would start the fire with magic, something he now did without any real concentration at all. The men would then go hunting, and if something was found it was butchered away from the camp, returned with just the meat and hides. The men ate the game they hunted, but if they needed to do so would supplement their meals from the pack horse supplies.

"Why don't you have your *drakon* hunt to help us out?" Miller asked Cylethe, once everyone was sitting around the fire. A foot of snow now coated the ground, but they had the uncured hides of previous kills that most men sat on. The rest sat on boxes from the pack horses since the pack animals had to be unloaded every night. Unloading allowed the horses to browse under the snow for grasses after a ration of oats.

Cylethe pointed toward the venison roasting on sticks over the fire. “You’re doing well enough to eat something.”

“Couldn’t we travel an hour or two longer if you hunted?” Miller persisted.

“My friend is not a pet,” she replied. “I don’t demand he serve me or others. He does so, if he wishes, as my friend, not a slave.”

“I thought you bought him,” Harry asked. “From a dragon? How does one even go about that?”

Cylethe’s eyes narrowed. “I suppose you can say it that way, but what I did was trade gold for the continued existence of my *drakon*. The things he does for me may stem from his knowledge of what I did for him, to some degree. But I think he feels we’re friends now as well.”

“But how do you go about it?” Miller asked. “Could I do it?”

“When dragons are with eggs, they pick out a cave that will suit them. Or other shelter, if need be, a hollowed-out castle will work well. The mother destroys the ground cover for a good distance so she can see any approaching dangers. That act, a circular dead zone, is indication that a dragon is nesting.

“I found such a place, far away from home, on the other side of the Aldikkis as I wandered the world. The dragon had numerous offers for her one dead egg when I arrived, but she looked at me and decided that I was her choice. I still don’t know why. I carried less gold than many others who sought the egg.”

Parker started to speak, but then seemed to think better of it.

"Go ahead," Cylethe demanded. "Out with it."

In Harry's opinion Parker could use more courage. Cylethe shouldn't intimidate him at this point. The man, however, seemed reluctant to talk to her.

"Your *drakon* doesn't look dead. Sickly maybe," Parker finally spat out.

"Dragons don't die in the sense that you and I do," Cylethe told him. "They are animated by a life force that we don't fully understand. Long after their bodies die and rot away their essence may still animate their bones, still wield their breath weapons, and still behave as they did in life."

"Aaaah," Miller said. "So the babies are dead, but they're still animated by their life force?"

"Not exactly," Cylethe told him. "Their bodies still have some life in them. But not enough to grow as a dragon grows. In time my *drakon*, whose name is Meluthian by the way, may die and become bones. Today he lives, breathes, and eats as you and I do. But he will never grow to be the dragon that his brood mates will. Regardless, he will still be my friend."

Miller nodded his understanding. "I think I see what you mean when you say Meluthian straddles life and death."

"Why don't the mother dragons just raise them?" Garrett asked. "Not too many mothers give up their babies."

"You're thinking in human terms," Cylethe replied. "And dek terms," she admitted after a pause. "But dragons don't rear any of their young. The normal ones can take care of themselves when they break the shell. The dead ones, like my *drakon*, can't. The mother actually wants to find someone who will properly take care of the dragon spirit that resides within."

"Too deep for me," Harry said. "I'm going to get some rest. Tomorrow we continue the climb, and I want to start more serious sword training with the men. We'll travel one hour less."

"We shouldn't do that," Cylethe said. "If we get caught in the winter storms—"

"Then we won't get caught. We move faster, so we can cut off early and train."

The men groaned.

Cylethe's expression indicated she didn't agree with that choice either.

Harry closed his eyes a minute, his face probably revealed his frustration. His men needed to train. They needed to be able to fight or they'd be dead when the bullets ran out.

"We'll march until we go as far as we went today," Harry offered. "I didn't see you complaining about that. I want us to move far enough, fast enough, so we can train."

The dek nodded her agreement.

Speaking to him without words from the scabbard on his back, Harry could sense the eagerness of *Dynamus* to train. It anticipated whatever came after the men being ready and able to fight.

The sense of contentedness that followed Harry's realization of that let him know he was on the right path as far as the sword was concerned. What lay in the future that would require fighting men? And men who were capable of sword combat?

Or did the sword even sense the future?

Time would tell.

Chapter 21 - Deep River

Irsu was no different than any other dwarf. He loved his wife; he wanted a family. He loved his Hold, his King, and his people.

Finding himself in the bottom of a river-cut cavern deep underground and back on Aerth was not part of his life plan. His soldiers, however, were the best of the best. While here he would serve them, and if needed, offer his life for them. He was not the dwarf he was five years earlier. Now he was a warrior and a commander of other warriors.

Which is what made the thought of where he was survivable. It was extremely unlikely he'd see Kordina again inside a year. Gates to Earth weren't simply laying around to be found. He knew of precisely two of them. The one in Iron Mountain Hold, and the large gate created and controlled by Hagirr that sat on the plains far south of his current location.

Hevreg would never let him back into Iron Mountain. The guardians of the Hagirr gate would question him, wondering how he got back to Aerth, a secret he could not reveal without betraying his people. The guardians may or may not let him return to Earth via that gate. He had no path that wasn't risky, including the river in front of him.

For the most part it was four to six hands deep, but occasionally it slowed and grew deeper. The walls as the edge of the river had an occasional sandbar they'd utilize to rest, but for the most part the river filled the ravine edge to edge, and they spent the majority of their time in the water. Numo, the only one of them that could swim, scouted ahead at the deep points to determine the safety of the far side, then the lizards would ferry the soldiers through the deep sections a few at a time.

Fortunately, that was rare. Most of the time the river was shallow and fast, dancing along through boulders and gravel.

He wondered what sort of fish lived here, and if they were edible, until Coragg interrupted.

"You're thinking again," Coragg chided him. "One foot in front of the other. It's the only way to get on down here."

"It's my job to think," Irsu replied. "I'm wondering how we're going to get back to Earth."

"I'm wondering what's around the next bend," Coragg countered. "You should be wondering the same. I've talked to Numo. He's never been down this particular ravine, although other scouts have. He tells me the scouts each have territories to cover, so they get very familiar with it. This wasn't his."

"So we're scouting now. We're fourteen of the best Iron Mountain has to offer," Irsu told his friend. "Whatever we find, we'll deal with it."

"We lost Horgra on our first encounter with an enemy. I think we're going to need to deal with it better."

"I don't disagree. You're my second. Help me."

Coragg gently clasped Irsu on the back. "I'm your brother in arms, and your brother in blood. I'm more than your second. If I don't get you home to Kordina, I'm not going home at all. Trust me, I'm helping you."

Irsu grinned and started to tease Coragg about getting all

mushy, but Numo returned from scouting and interrupted.

The scout was soaked to the bone. From his breathing it was clear he was tired. "Our journey eases thirty *dokadros* ahead. Someone has cut a road into the cavern wall on the right side facing downriver, wide enough for the pack lizards and for fighting if need be. While not Dwarven, they did a good job, all the rock they cut is gone. Moved somewhere else."

"That's several days of travel for these lizards, Numo, you move fast. Does the water get deeper again or did you decide it was bath day?" Coragg asked.

"Bath day," Numo answered. "Definitely bath day. I slipped on a rock."

Irsu couldn't see well enough to tell using the darkness vision that every dwarf was born with, but he assumed Numo was blushing. A slipping scout was much like a sword-dropping soldier.

But it happened, even to the best at times, and they were all under duress.

"Ride on one of the lizards for a while," he ordered. "Pick one, relieve the handler. When you're dry, you can rejoin me and we'll talk."

"One more thing. There is a mushwood stand on the left side of the river half the distance to the road. A sandy copse where we can make a camp and rest if you like, Commander. Fire would be welcome in my bones."

"And in mine," Irsu agreed. "We'll camp there tonight, have some food. Did you see anything edible?"

"Rats, small lizards, some mushrooms. Make a good stew, and it's better than dried rations. If the rations are still dry and even edible, that is."

"They should be," Coragg said. "The lizards are handling the river better than we are."

Numo nodded and headed toward his prize, a dry seat.

"What do you think?" Coragg asked Irsu.

"If the oasis looks safe, we camp. Maybe a day, maybe longer depending on the condition of the men. Water doesn't do our feet any good."

"Wise."

"When we're rested, we'll make for the road. We'll take some mushwood with us to burn so we can dry out once again when we get there."

"Mordain provides," Coragg said. "And we fight for his people."

Irsu shrugged. "Or we just got lucky. I've never seen proof the gods give a damn."

Coragg scowled. "Someday, my friend, battle will make you a believer."

"You may be right. That day hasn't come yet."

They arrived at the mushwood stand just as the dwarves were starting to complain about being tired. Even the royal guard had a limit. The stand was everything Irsu had hoped for and more. At some point the river had cut into the wall, creating a loaf-shaped opening five *kadros* long that had filled with sand as the river abandoned the undercut to take another course. Large rocks poked up through the sand, creating a very defensible terrain if the sickly dwarves were pursuing them and caught up.

The game situation was even better than Numo reported. Even as Irsu looked, a blind cave hare darted from the river water onto the shore. Probably surviving by eating moss from the river bottom, the clean vegetation fed hare would be a tasty treat. And where there was one, there were more, such was the nature of hares.

Mushwood rose from the sand in a dozen small copses, plenty of wood for burning and even building something they might need if a thought of such a thing arose.

Then such a thought came to him. A way to stay dry and reduce the maintenance of their armor.

"Coragg, do you think we could build a raft to use on this river?"

Chapter 22 - A Delicate Balance

Elianna woke next to Hagirr, and only him. Throughout their centuries together they'd often shared their bed with beautiful slaves, worthy diplomats, or an occasional fetish race. When decades dragged on into centuries, and then into millennia, it benefited sanity to refresh a relationship with the exotic.

But she'd just returned home after some time away. Therefore it was just the two of them, and they renewed the bond between them that neither shared with anyone else.

"Is it time to get out of bed already?" Hagirr complained.

"No, we need to talk," she replied. "You're going about Ernst the wrong way."

He rubbed his eyes and sat up amid the cascade of pillows on the palatial bed. "Feeding him the dinner of his life was wrong?"

"When you mix it with the subtle terror you inflicted on him and his wife." Elianna grasped Hagirr's hand and squeezed. "You're the human. They are impressed that it is one of their own that leads this world. In fact, in the Germany I told you about, they couldn't imagine anything else."

"Neither could I," Hagirr confessed.

"What I'm saying, dearest Hagirr, is that Ernst and Herta imagine themselves every bit as superior as you do. I've taught them to fear what we can do, you have to show them what we can offer." She shook her head. "I'm concerned with your comment. The one that they haven't seen a thing yet. If you intend to show them only fear, that will not work."

“It always works,” Hagirr protested, “and I don’t know why I should need or care about this Germany anyway.”

“Because they really are a smaller example of what you’ve built on Aerth. They will work with you if they see themselves in you. If you scare them, they will die for the ‘Fatherland’ they are so proud of.”

Hagirr laughed, and pulled her to him, resting her head on his chest. “They haven’t seen the gates to the hells yet. Once they do, the thought of death will hold more fear than the thought of living with my wishes.”

Elianna slapped his hand. Of all the creatures in existence on two worlds, only she was capable of treating Hagirr as her total equal. She did as he bade, but her counsel was the only honest advisement he got.

“Show them that magic is good. That it is a power to make their lives better, and to make the lives of Germany better. If you can do that, they will serve you until the end of their existence.”

“What do you have in mind?” he asked.

“I’ll leave that for you to decide, my love, but I can tell you what we must have.”

“What?”

“There is a device called the Ark of the Covenant. It is an artifact that will close your precious gate and Ernst was looking for it with the intention to use it. We must stop Germany from seeking that end. We must enlist them on our side to keep the Hagirr gate open.”

“What is this Ark of the Coveting?”

"Covenant. That's a promise between a god and mortals."

"Covenant then," he replied. "Why should I care about this Ark?"

"It's a barrier, designed to keep gates from opening on Earth, and created by a god left there after the fracture. It was supposed to stop you from rejoining the worlds. While its power seems to have weakened, Ernst thinks it can close gates that have managed to open."

"Well the Earth god won't be the first to have failed," he said, laughing. "Where is this lost god now?"

"Just that. Lost."

"And the Ark?"

"Hidden, but I will find and destroy it. I will put Ernst and his wife Herta in place as leaders of this Germany, and they will help you gather humans into the gate. They think they deserve to rule their world, and if all other human races are gone, they feel that Earth is the better for it."

"Then, once Earth has only Germany left, we can sweep them up last," Hagirr said.

"Sparing Ernst and Herta, but yes. As for those two, I've grown fond of them."

"Pets?"

"Companions," she rebutted. "I have given them my word."

"How unlike you," Hagirr said, laughing more. "Elianna is growing maternal after so many centuries."

She pulled away from him and glared. “Hardly. I simply feel their service deserves some reward, better than what’s in store for the rest of humanity.”

“You will have it as you wish,” he said. “It is no loss if two humans do not feed the soul stone. We will have more than enough. If that is the case, we can release the excess back onto the plains to serve us at some point in the future.”

“Germany will help us see to that vision,” Elianna agreed. “But spare these two for me.”

“Love me, and it is done.”

Elianna smiled. It was always satisfying to get her way from the unpredictable Hagirr. But if he gave his word to her, he never broke it. She looked over at the servants. “You will all leave us until the sun is high. The humans are to be well fed, and given a chance to tour the gardens. Have them waiting for us at noon out front, with carriages ready to take us to the pyramids.”

“Your will, my lady,” an elven woman said as she bowed.

She spent a good part of the morning reminding Hagirr why he loved her, and just precisely why he would be best served to remember her wishes.

Chapter 23 - The Great Pyramid of Jangik

July 19, 1940

Ernst rose early, as did Herta. Neither of them slept very well. While the bed was extremely comfortable, the room at the perfect temperature, and the quiet unbroken, the world was definitely still alien to them and a twinge of danger lingered in their minds.

The air smelled wrong. Maybe it was alien flowers, maybe the composition of the air itself was different than Earth.

“Ernst, I would be lying if I said I wasn’t scared,” Herta said, joining him beside massive glass doors that opened onto a veranda.

He led her outside, where they sat on furniture perfect in its design and execution. White wicker, it had not a single flaw. It contoured to them perfectly as they sat across a short table of similar construction.

Apparently, their rise from sleep did not go unnoticed. A servant appeared in the doorway and waited for them to notice her. Thin, nearly translucent skin of alabaster, the female wasn’t human. She was at least as diminutive as Elianna and seemed far more vulnerable.

“Lord, lady, do you wish to have breakfast on the veranda?” the creature asked.

“What manner of being are you?” Herta blurted out.

“I am a mountain elf,” the servant asked, unphased by either Herta’s question or demeanor.

Ernst leapt in. “We’d love breakfast…” he paused, as if waiting for a name, gesturing with his hands to indicate the servant should speak.

“You may call me Mallah, Lord. I will serve you in your quarters while you are in the palace.”

“Mallah. We’d love breakfast. Surprise us with what you like most.”

“As the lord wishes,” Mallah replied, bowing. A second later she was gone.

Ernst turned to Herta. “Luxury. This is luxury, yet we are both frightened, my dear. Everything comes with a price.”

“What price are we to pay?” Herta asked, her eyes plaintive.

“I don’t know. I haven’t been disarmed,” he told her. “Either they don’t fear my Luger, or they have no idea what it is. Rest assured, if they threaten you, I will use it.”

“And we’ll die together,” his wife retorted. “Use your wits first. Use the Luger to make sure they pay a price if they intend to harm us.”

“I don’t feel Elianna was entirely happy with Hagirr last night. I saw a look of displeasure on her face with him, particularly when he pulled that trick with the living plant.”

She shuddered. “That thing deserved to die. I just didn’t want it near me.”

“But it was tasty,” Ernst said. “I just don’t know if we were eating a thinking creature or not.”

“Does it matter?” she replied. “Why does this Hagirr, if he’s all powerful, surround himself with inhuman monstrosities?”

"I don't know," Ernst said, gesturing toward the door. Mallah had returned.

"Lord, lady, I have brought you a breakfast served in the mountains," the servant said. "Roast ram, potatoes, *tengeski*, and *portlue*."

With the aid of another servant, she sat two large silver platters in front of them. A meat, shredded and fried potatoes, and what looked like a deep purple boiled egg. A bowl of something curdled was sat next to the platters.

"*Tengeski*?" Ernst asked, pointing at the egg.

"Yes," Mallah replied, sitting utensils on the table. "The egg of a large bird found in the mountains I was born in."

"Is that far?" Herta asked.

"Oh yes, many months on horse or wagon."

"Then how do the eggs get here fresh?" Herta pressed.

Mallah laughed. "*Tengeski* is not fresh, lady. It is fermented under cold sand for at least a year. These eggs are from the *Tengesk* birds in Lord Hagirr's zoo, so if they were to be eaten fresh, that would not be a problem."

Herta looked at the egg on her plate, several times the size of a chicken egg, and turned a shade of green.

Mallah gave Ernst and Herta a napkin, then disappeared through the veranda doors without a sound. She was either to be seen as little as possible as a direction from her superiors, or that was how she did her job on her own directive. Ernst suspected that if he said her name, she'd appear quickly.

"This is barbaric," Herta said to Ernst, pointing at the egg. "We're to eat rotten food?"

"Eat the sheep, and the potatoes," Ernst replied. "I suspect we'll need a strong constitution today. Please, dear, show no weakness to our hosts. They need to believe Germany is their equal, not that we are any less strong than they are."

"We've killed their dragons," Herta retorted. "They should not believe us weak!"

"Ssshhh!" Ernst stood and looked over the balcony. Verdant gardens spread out below, no sign of anyone listening. But he had no idea what the limitations of magic were. Surely they were monitored. Returning to his seat, he smiled at his wife. "My dear, a diplomat you are not. Please. No weakness, but no insult either. Choose your words carefully or do not speak."

"Germany is not weak," Herta growled. She took a spoon from the table and dug out a large bite of the *tengeski*. Staring Ernst in the eye, she put the bite in her mouth, chewed, and swallowed.

The sour look on her face disappeared as she tilted her head and smiled.

"That is delicious!" she remarked.

Ernst tried it. It was. He picked up some of the other food, from the bowl. It looked like cheese, but it had what seemed to be clear-ish worms living in it. He breathed deeply then stuffed a curd into his mouth.

Also delicious.

“Try the curds but don’t look too close,” Ernst said. “Equally delightful to the egg.” As his wife smiled with joy at the taste, he sighed deeply. “What is to be said of this place, Herta? I feel a threat looming, yet it is almost paradise as we sit here.”

“We live each moment,” Herta finally replied after her third bite from her plate. Whatever they show us today, whatever intimidation or bribery they use, we stand strong for the interest of Germany. Elianna is terrifying. I feel this Hagirr’s heart is even more cruel.”

Ernst rose again and sat on his wife’s chair with her. He kissed her and then pulled her close, intending to whisper in her ear. “Whatever you do, do not mention the Ark,” Ernst said. “Elianna hasn’t mentioned it for a very long time, and it is best she remains unconcerned.”

Herta squeezed his hand, indicating she understood. “You know, at first I loved your power,” she told him. “But now I feel I love you as well. You love Germany as much as I do.”

“We both feel it, I agree,” Ernst told her. “Despite the actions of our countrymen, the intolerable fools, the selfish sycophants, we are rising above it. We, Herta, you and I, we hold Germany in our hands. More than any Führer, more than Himmler or anyone like him.”

She rose and took his hand and led him back through the glass doors. “No matter what the rest of our day holds, I will love you now.”

It was nearly noon when a servant came for them. They were provided clothes to wear, comfortable and non-restrictive, Ernst felt strange dressing outside of his normal attire. Herta, however, looked amazing. Like a princess from Scandinavian mythology.

Dressed, fed, and energized, they were led to the front steps of the palace compound, where several open top carriages waited. Unlike the night before, strange creatures were in the air as well. Men, or rather elves, rode fantastical beasts that seemed a mix of creatures. Graceful winged horses were the most normal, but there were also creatures he recognized from the superstitious past of Europe. Griffins, with the heads of eagles and the bodies of lions zoomed overhead in complex patterns, each carrying a rider with either a bow or a lance.

There was a third kind with the front of an eagle, but where the eagle's tail would be the body of a horse, or at least the back half, resided.

Two other beasts seemed to be all bird, but their feathers smoldered with fire, leaving thin black smoke as they passed through the air. When they opened their mouths to screech, fire burned a bright orange deep in their throats. No rider adorned these, but Ernst noticed they closely followed two different female riders on winged horses.

"That's a pegasus," Mallah told him as she noticed him staring. "The creature following is imprinted on the rider. It's a raptor from Acheron."

"Acheron?" Ernst asked.

"A place of torment, where an evil one can wind up after death depending on the nature of the evil."

Ernst shivered, despite the comfortable climate of Jangik. It seemed even the servants would remind him of the tortures that await in the afterlife should he fail as a human being.

"This is your carriage," Mallah indicated. "I can ride with

you as your guide, or walk behind if that is your pleasure."

"Please, be our guide," Herta said.

So much for any chance to speak to his wife without listening ears. But no matter, the carriage driver might be a spy as well. He'd find a way to speak to her later if they needed to discuss the events of this day in privacy.

The three of them climbed into the carriage just as Hagirr and Elianna exited the front doors of the palace. A host of guards formed a semi-circle ahead of them, all the same race of elf as Elianna.

Ernst wondered if that was the race of elf Hagirr considered Aryan. What did she call herself? A desert elf. If indeed the planet Aerth followed the same ideology as Germany, there would be racial winners and losers.

He placed little stock in such thinking. The worth of a person was determined by their intellect and actions, not the color of their eyes. But as long as it was the prevailing opinion in seats of power, he was pragmatic enough to go along.

"Mallah, I notice all the guards are the same race as Elianna. Is there a reason?"

"Lady Elianna's tribe is favored. It's said that when Lord Hagirr rose to power that Elianna was at his side, destroying his enemies. That her family and tribe swore allegiance, delivering his power out into a world broken into chaos."

"I see," he replied. "They've proved themselves."

"Unlike my people, who opposed the Lord. We now are bound to servitude until such a time as a hero arises to prove our worth, erasing the shame we bear for our shortsightedness."

"A hero?"

"Someone to redeem the honor of the mountain elves, my Lord." She tilted her head, and he couldn't help but feel she thought what she was explaining to be an elementary concept that a child should know. "Now that the Joining of Worlds is underway, such a hero may arise. When he or she does, we will be liberated into full citizens."

Ernst nodded. The mountain elves would never have such a hero. But hope is what kept them in servitude, hope that they'd somehow be redeemed. Hagirr was smart. He chose to make his subjects cooperative instead of destroying their spirit.

As he and Mallah finished their conversation, Hagirr and Elianna took seats in a different carriage. The procession began moving. Citizens of Jangik lined the streets, and many threw flowers or paper artwork into the path of their tyrant. Several times he recognized the word 'human' uttered from the lips of those they passed. He couldn't tell if it was in adulation or mockery without understanding the surrounding words to associate with the smiles.

He leaned toward Herta. "Elianna wasn't lying. This world is almost precisely like Germany."

"It's glorious," she responded, smiling and waving at the beings they passed.

"Yes. Glorious."

Several minutes later they arrived at the pyramid that seemed so important here. Ernst could see why, it was an amazing structure that likely dwarfed the pyramids in Egypt, although he'd never seen them to be sure.

Guards helped Herta down from the carriage, Ernst followed, then finally Mallah. One of the guards handed Ernst a belt with a small scabbard and knife on it. The pommel of the knife glistened, almost as if it had its own light within.

"Why do I need this?" Ernst asked, feeling for his Luger under his clothing.

"It is enchanted," a guard answered, holding a gold medallion in his hands. The same one he now noticed Mallah wore. A cult perhaps?

"But why do I need it?" Ernst pressed.

"All warriors come into the pyramid armed, Lord. You are a warrior, yes?"

Ernst thought about his answer. What would benefit him?

"Yes, I am a warrior."

"Then wear it with honor." The guard helped Ernst strap the blade to his waist.

Hagirr and Elianna joined them. "I trust you had an excellent morning?" Hagirr asked.

"We did," Herta answered him. "Thank you for your hospitality. We've never been in a place like this."

Ernst nodded his agreement.

"I see you wear a warrior's blade," Hagirr said to Ernst. "Then we are ready to enter the pyramid, the four of us."

A larger wagon pulled up some distance away. Enclosed, the back door was chained. Barred windows, three to a side, allowed air inside so something or someone could breathe. A hand suddenly grasped one of the bars, and it looked remarkably human. The sleeve of the shirt or tunic the owner of the hand wore reminded Ernst of something he'd seen before.

He was distracted as four winged beasts landed by them. A griffin and three of the winged horses.

"Our rides to the platform above," Hagirr said. "Please, lady, allow me to help you," the man said as he assisted Herta up into the saddle of one of the beasts." He secured her in place with a belt. "Ernst, that one is yours. The griffin is mine, he's been imprinted on me since he was hatched ten years ago, otherwise I'd let you ride him."

"I'm most enamored of this beast," Ernst replied, approaching the pegasus Hagirr had gestured toward. "I'm honored to ride him."

"The pegasi are much more intelligent," Elianna explained. "You can speak to them; they will understand you. The griffin my Lord rides is more of an animal, he responds to Hagirr solely from training and love."

Hagirr leapt into the saddle of his beast, which immediately took to the air in sweeping wing beats. The three pegasi followed, apparently knowing what to do. The wizard had mentioned that the ride would be to the platform Ernst could see far up the face of the pyramid, but he took a long route to get there. They swept out over the city, revealing the splendor of Jangik to the two Germans.

It was marvelous. City buildings, probably government centers, temples, and forums interspersed with estates and houses that Berliners would sell their first born to live in. Canals traced through the city; at the high walls the water was lifted in gigantic buckets to spill out into the rivers that bordered the city. Other bucket lifts drew fresh water into the canals at different points. Roads, paved with perfectly cut stones, allowed citizens to move freely.

Inside the expansive walls the city was beautiful. Ernst saw buildings outside the walls in the distance, but they didn't fly there to get a good view. Large gates rested on the walls at the ends of larger roads within the city, and he noticed that outside the city walls the roads shot straight as an arrow toward the horizon.

Finally, they returned to the pyramid, landing on the platform Hagirr had spoken of earlier. Two dozen of Elianna's people stood in a semi-circle as they landed.

After they dismounted the four great beasts flew off together, apparently returning to where they came from to wait until Hagirr summoned them for a return to the ground.

Ernst looked out over the edge of the platform, which had no railings. It dropped off ten meters to the slope of the pyramid, which looked as if it was made of white ice. Getting down from here without an aerial ride, or getting here without one, would be problematic.

"This way," Elianna told them. The elf turned to face the others of her kind, then ran to embrace one. "Mother!" she exclaimed, kissing a female that looked even younger than Elianna.

After exchanging gestures of affection with the other elf while Hagirr looked on with disdain, Elianna turned to him.

"Mother, this is Ernst and Herta Haufmann, of Earth. They

are the future of our bond with the human world."

Elianna's mother looked at them with much the same disdain as Hagirr looked at his mother-in-law.

"A pleasure, I'm sure," the elf replied.

"This is my mother, Sylinth," Elianna said to Ernst and Herta.

"Lady Sylinth," her mother corrected.

"Lady Sylinth, the pleasure is ours," Ernst said, aware this female had some pull with Elianna. If he wanted to see Earth again with his wife, it was important not to offend.

"The hallways are ready for your tour," Sylinth said to Hagirr. "Why you waste your time, I don't know."

"It is my time to waste," Hagirr replied. "And yours to obey."

That clearly irritated Sylinth, which amused Ernst. He kept that to himself.

"This way," Hagirr said, gesturing toward an opening into the pyramid. "We have much to see."

Chapter 24 - Brest

July 19, 1940

Brest was on fire.

"Mother of God," Gunter whispered.

Nelson grabbed his field glasses and scanned the town. Deaders walked the streets, and vast numbers of soldiers stood in pens on the edges of the town. A circle of deaders stood like a wall around the city as patrols of the creatures searched for more of the living. A line of deaders pushed a few dozen men dressed in US Army uniforms ahead of them down the street. If the men resisted, the dead shredded them on the spot. The living soon learned to accept being herded.

A column of smoke rose from an airfield on the north of the city, a few hundred planes in molten ruins. The dragons had been here, and not long ago.

Several dozen ships burned in the bay, sunk to the bottom with various portions of the decks sticking out above the water. Much of the infrastructure was melted slag.

The carnage below was complete. The USA had been not only routed, but utterly defeated, at least in France. Nelson wondered if the stuffed suits in Washington DC knew about this yet.

He sat and pondered his next steps.

"There's nothing we can do here," he finally said. "Crawl back through the brush, then we can stand and march away unseen on the other side."

"We can't just leave," Private Connors said.

"We are leaving," Nelson told him.

"We have to do something," Connors insisted. "Those are our people."

"We ain't doing squat," Nelson replied, turning to face the kid while pulling his cigar from his mouth to spit. "You go down there and you'll be in a pen or torn apart."

"We can't just sit here!"

Nelson had heard of men on the edge, and Connors was there. Gunter's face showed he saw it too.

"Boy, you can go down there if you like," Gunter said. "You'll be defying orders, but we won't shoot you. Leave most of your stuff here and do what you like."

"We all have to go," Connors said, pleading. Tears started to roll down his cheeks. "That's how we were supposed to get home."

"It ain't happening like that," Nelson told him, as he stood up on the east side of the bushes. He looked at Gunter. "We make for Calais, acquire a boat, cross the channel and hope we make it."

"Sounds like a plan," the other sergeant agreed. "Long walk."

"We daren't take a truck," Nelson said. "We won't make ten miles."

"Agreed."

The other men stood up as well, even Connors.

"We're going to get home, Connors," Nelson said, resting his hand on the private's back. "You need to keep it together so

Sergeant Gunter and I can make that happen."

"I'm fine now," the kid assured him.

Nelson nodded. He believed the private, his insubordination seemed to be a moment of desperation. Nelson looked at his companions. "Then we go back the same path we came. It seemed safe enough the first time around. We return to the supply depot and restock for our trip to Calais. We walk until dark, then we hole up in some farmhouse overnight. Billy, you understand?"

The big guy nodded and pointed east, not breaking his streak of silence. Not that it mattered. He didn't ever say more than one word anyway.

"Close enough," Nelson said.

The trudge away from Brest had to be the most demoralizing moment of his life. There were originally tens of thousands of soldiers at the American camps in the French city. Now there was a fraction of that number in pens erected by the dead. That his men could do nothing but walk away sapped them of their self-respect, of their morale, and of their faith.

"God's kept us free and alive for a reason," Nelson told them. "Believe in Him and you'll get to safety. He has a plan for us."

Nobody said a word. He had no way of knowing if they believed it or not.

Billy clamped his massive paw on Nelson's shoulder and squeezed slightly. Nelson looked up into the man's face, and whatever had broken Billy down to a near mute hadn't robbed his spirit. The man was ready to fight if that's what it took to get to Calais. Nelson didn't see a man with a fractured mind.

He saw a soldier.

Taking his hand from Nelson's shoulder, Billy clenched it into a fist and shook it once in a sharp downward motion, toward the east, while nodding his head once.

As if to say, "Let's get this done."

Billy had faith.

And where there was one, there was salvation.

Chapter 25 – Slaughter

The next day Harry and the squad set out with every intention of covering more ground than the day before. The stop to speak to the Flitterboots had cost them time, and now their new discovery would cost them even more.

A beastly scene of slaughter.

"Gnolls," Cylethe said.

"Dog men," Miller replied.

"They're called gnolls. That bigger one over there is a flind," she corrected. "Whatever their reason, they fought to the death here against our people."

Harry couldn't help but notice Cylethe had said 'our'. She considered the humans to be her kin now, and kin to the Dek.

"Miller, you count the dead gnolls," Harry ordered. "Hans, you count the dead dek. Lars, Parker, after Hans counts them you gather the dek and line them up here," he pointed to a stout pine tree, "in a row. We will give an accounting to Grandmother. Cylethe will decide what needs be done here."

"If the survivors didn't burn them, it's because more danger was nearby," Cylethe told him. "We should burn them to free their spirits, but you should get your guards in position. Looking in all directions, even up."

"Why don't you scout from the sky?" Harry suggested.

"I will, closer to dark, after we've moved on from this place.

Right now, I'd be seen. The pyre we need to build will attract attention for some distance, so we won't light that until we're ready to leave. The smell of the dead will attract predators. We don't want to stay here too long."

Harry nodded and assigned all but three of his men to guard duty. He kept Jenkins and Burke with him. "Okay, you two, we're the worker bees. We gather wood for the pyre."

He passed out axes from the pack horses, and they got to work. It took a good part of their day, but they finished three hours before sundown. Fortunate timing, as they'd have an hour to travel and two more to set up their camp that night in a defensible fashion. He had no way of knowing if the forty dead gnolls they counted would have brothers seeking vengeance on the dek.

Miller lit the pyre when it was ready, after eighteen dead Undek warriors were laid across it. It was the best they could do.

Ten minutes later the pyre was burning, and black smoke rose into the sky.

"We have to go," Harry said. "That's a beacon for any around who might mean us harm."

A grueling mile and a half later, climbing trail that seemed increasingly steep, they selected a good section of trail to camp. Sheer rock face was on the east side of their path, and a sharp downward slope on the west. Anything that came at them would either have to come down the cliff from above or use the small section of traversable ground. Anything coming up from below would be easy to destroy. The high ground meant everything in a world like this one.

"The weather favors us," Cylethe told him. "Tonight will be

brutally cold." She gestured at a snowflake drifting past her face. "And worsening snow will be here soon after dark. Maybe before."

He didn't ask her how she knew the weather would worsen. She didn't seem to be wrong very often.

The twelve trekkers set up three tents around a center firepit, packing down the thin snow floors before covering them with pine boughs. Two men shared a bed, it was how they retained warmth.

Cylethe indicated quite forcefully that none of the men would share her bed, not even Miller. With one exception.

"You may share my bed, Harry. It is always warm, I assure you."

He blushed as the men laughed. It was remarkable how quickly they'd come to accept her. "My wife's bed would never be warm again," he replied. "You understand that I have vows to another."

"Otherwise he'd be keeping warmer than an'body 'ere," Lars offered up to the laughter of the other men.

The sorceress shrugged. "Shame. Then I sleep alone."

The men might have accepted her, if she offered, despite her magic, despite her tattoos, despite her filed teeth. But Harry noticed none of them made the suggestion to take his spot.

"Lars, Garrett, you're first watch. Two hours. One of you watches up the trail, one down. Both keep an eye on the cliff face. Use the skins from the hunts to keep warm, it's already getting colder. Wake the normal rotation to follow."

"Aye," they answered. "Least we're not in the deep night."

"That's me and Miller," Harry told them. "Two watches from now. Eyes open, you know how dangerous it is here."

Harry, uncomfortable with the arrangements, slipped into the furs with Miller. Cylethe, who shared their tent, stripped nude and lay on top of the furs on her bed.

"It's getting colder," he told her. "You should cover yourself."

"Something isn't right," she said. "I will be ready; furs will slow me down. Meluthian watches overhead, in the darkness. I will wake you if there is trouble."

Harry shook his head. "Nothing is going to be out in this weather. And you're going to catch a cold. Besides, Miller is uncomfortable seeing you nude."

Miller gasped. "I am no—"

Harry clamped his hand over the radioman's mouth. "He's a gentleman, he'd never admit to it, of course."

Cylethe leaned up on her elbow and looked at Harry. "Nudity is not of any significance among my people, Harry. I'm sensing that among yours it is? Or are you reconsidering my offer?"

Truth was the offer was tempting. Cylethe wasn't pretty by any means, no, just the opposite. But she was confident, powerful, and for some reason her demeanor suited Harry just fine. He had no doubt she knew it. His struggle was to resist temptation.

"I am not," Harry protested. "Although I don't wish you to

take offense over it."

"None taken," she said, laughing. "Your loss, trust me."

Damn her. He was happy to be sleeping in his clothes, at least. His temptation wouldn't be so obvious. He laid his head down in the furs and closed his eyes.

Then opened them what seemed like a moment later.

A bright light illuminated the camp outside the tent flap. Men were shouting. In more than one language. He slipped his boots on without lacing them and grabbed his crossbow before racing out of the tent. Several of his men stood in a circle around a vertical line of arcing light about twenty feet from the campfire, on the uptrail side. The line rose twenty feet into the sky.

Cylethe joined him, still nude. "A gateway seam. We need to be ready."

Miller walked up next to her.

"Ready the Fire Lance spell I taught you," she ordered him. "When I say, cast it into the gate. *Only* if I tell you to."

The line suddenly and violently opened into a rectangle twenty feet high and thirty wide. Part of it hung out over the slope below.

Harry could see through it. People were on the other side, in a stone hallway.

"Hagirr," Cylethe growled, then began casting.

A young human male, no more than his early twenties, stood on the other side with an elf female. Other figures behind them were less focused, apparently being further away from the gate mattered to how much detail one could see.

"I am Hagirr, yes," the young man said, speaking to them from the other side of the gate. "I want the Templar-wizard."

"Take aim!" Harry ordered his men. Rifles rose to the ready, pointed at the gate. For a moment Harry thought he heard the exclamation of a German woman on the other side.

"Stand ready," Cylethe ordered Miller. "Roll the syllables, as I taught you."

Miller was chanting something. His hands glowed a baleful orange, as if power sat uncomfortably beneath the skin.

"Not today, wizard," Cylethe replied to Hagirr.

"I see you're teaching him," Hagirr said. "I'll correct your mistakes when I take him from you, dek whore."

The elf with him laughed, and her own hands began to glow as her lips moved rhythmically.

Hagirr put his hands on hers, stopping the spell. "We can't risk killing the Templar, dearest. For now the whore can keep him." He looked back toward Cylethe. "I doubt she intends to eat him. But she will have to die for defying me."

Hagirr waved his hands and the gate vanished in a burst of blue sparks.

For fifteen seconds everything was silent except for the wind and Miller's chant. Cylethe stopped him much as Hagirr had stopped the elf.

“Stand down,” Harry ordered his men. “Return to your watch schedule.” He looked at Cylethe. “How did he know where to find us?”

“He’s sensed Miller,” she replied. “The youngster doesn’t know how to hide his power yet.”

“What does that mean?”

Cylethe looked at him and thought a moment before answering. For the first time Harry saw fear in her eyes. “It means Hagirr will be watching us. He will come for Miller when he thinks we are vulnerable, and we will have to be ready if we want to have even a sliver of a chance at living.”

Chapter 26 - The Hall of Gates

July 19, 1940

"My first gift to you today, dear friends, are these." Hagirr waved his hand and two of the guards handed golden amulets to Ernst and Herta. "Wear them, you'll be able to understand any spoken language and others will understand you as well. They are yours to keep."

Ernst and Herta put them on, he spoke to her in French, she said it sounded like German to her. Fantastic gifts. "Will they work on Earth?" Herta asked.

"I assume so," Elianna told her, "mine does."

"Let's turn here," Hagirr said. He waved his hand at a section of wall adorned with carved images much like any other. The stone vanished as if it were never there.

"Amazing," Herta said. "More secure than any door."

"Indeed, lady," Hagirr replied. "This is but the first of many wonders you will see today."

Herta's grin was a mile wide, her fear from the last evening replaced with wonder. Ernst struggled valiantly to match her demeanor. He didn't want his host to think him ungrateful, and certainly didn't want Hagirr to think he didn't trust the wizard.

They passed a series of what looked like empty picture frames. Most of the walls in this hall were also carved, but inside the picture frames was flat stone. The frames, some sort of metal, extended floor to ceiling.

"This one," Hagirr told them. "I'd like you to see the plane of existence we call Acheron."

"That's from Greek mythology," Ernst said. "The river Acheron, in Hades, the flow of pain."

"Maybe someone in your ancient world actually saw the place," Elianna said. "It's possible to travel from Earth to Acheron."

"That is a possibility," Ernst agreed.

Hagirr danced an awkward dance in front of the frame, waving his fingers and chanting in words that felt evil and dangerous. Whatever language it was, the amulet translated none of it.

The frame flickered, then shimmered silverish like liquid mercury. A moment later the silver color turned to an image.

A red sky sat angrily over a blackened landscape. Volcanoes erupted in the distance, feeding black clouds that rained ash down on the land. Streaks of smoke littered the air, but the scene had an orderliness to it.

Until Hagirr moved the picture closer to the ground. At first it seemed as if insects covered the landscape, a series of rolling hills, but as the image drew even closer the skittering insects resolved into fighting creatures. Humans, dwarves, elves, and a host of other less seemly beings. Great machines of war hurled stones into enemy lines, many of the munitions on fire and trailing smoke.

Two great armies clashed. As men and creatures died their bodies vanished, leaving their gear to rattle empty to the soil. On both sides the combatants pressed forward, eager to earn their fate.

"The armies fighting here come from warrior cultures. For

some this is Hell, and only great bravery can redeem them into a place of reward. For others this is Heaven, they fight until they die, then return to feasting halls full of ale and women. The next day they fight again." Hagirr spat at the frame, and to Ernst's surprise the spit went through to be lost in the wind that blew on the other side. "Barbarians, all of them."

"Why show us this?" Ernst asked.

"Two reasons. The first is to let you know that this is where I banish my enemies. And as my friends, if you have need, I can banish your greatest enemies here as well."

The threat of Acheron was better than work camps, Ernst felt. And an effective yet unspoken threat from Hagirr to keep Ernst and Herta in line.

"The second is that I have a gift for your lovely wife and I can only find it here."

What manner of reward would be found in a land of the damned?

Elianna giggled. A very disarming and melodic sound. "Hagirr, you honor her beyond what she has earned!"

Herta frowned at Elianna, who smiled and waved a hand, dismissing Herta in a jovial manner.

Hagirr gestured with his hands and the image moved again. "Nonsense. You picked these two. I will honor them as trusted friends."

Ernst looked at Elianna. "If we're now trusted friends, then I have a question for you. When you found us you told me you wanted to find the Ark of the Covenant to close the gate." He lowered his face in a look of accusation. "That was never your plan, was it?"

She smiled at him. "Forgive me, Ernst, but I had to know the sort of man you were. Closing the gate would be a terrible mistake for you, for Germany, for Aerth."

"If we had found the Ark?" Ernst asked.

"I would have destroyed it. Killing you if you stood in the way."

Ernst nodded. He understood such tactics. "Well done."

Elianna curtsied, a remarkably human gesture. "A compliment from the future ruler of Earth."

He studied her face for sarcasm. Seeing none he asked her, "What do you mean?"

"She and I will discuss this with you later," Hagirr admonished. "But it suffices to say that you've made friends wisely, Ernst Hoffmann."

Friends he was certain kept him and Herta alive because they needed something. But if it benefited the Hoffmanns, then it was something that might happen. Ernst could be practical.

"Aha," Hagirr cried out. "I've found one."

The image was now underground, Ernst hadn't followed it during the conversation, so he didn't know how they'd arrived there. He was looking at a cavern wall now, however, and a small ledge jutted outward. A nest of sorts, made from bones, rested on the small flat surface.

Hagirr drew the image closer.

A baby bird lay in the bone pile, a severed arm of some creature lay next to it partially eaten.

"An Acheron raptor," Elianna whispered.

One of the creatures Ernst had seen flaming in the sky? Outrageous!

"Reach through and get it Herta," Hagirr told Ernst's wife. "It must imprint on you and you alone. Use these."

One of Elianna's relatives handed Herta a glove that looked to be made of asbestos, and a pillow made of the same material.

"I can just reach through?" Herta asked. "Look what the beast did to that arm."

"It is resting," Hagirr explained. "When it opens its eyes, you must be the first eyes it looks into. It will imprint immediately." He shrugged. "Of course, if you don't want it then I can—"

"No! I want it." Herta slipped on the glove and quickly reached for the bird.

"Gently," Elianna counseled.

Herta put her fingers around the bird and gently lifted it. The fledgling, tired, lay its head down on the glove material. She carefully lifted it and brought it back through the frame. She lay the bird, gently and with great care, on the pillow that was offered to her.

"Name it," Hagirr advised.

"Adolf," Herta purred. "I name it Adolf."

Ernst rolled his eyes.

"What?" Herta scowled. "If not for Herr Hitler you and I would not have met, and you'd do well to remember that. He may be dead, but he cared for the Fatherland as I do."

"Of course, dear," Ernst said, pacifying her. Hitler was a madman and a psychopath. But he was also dead, and Ernst didn't care to shatter Herta's illusions on the topic.

The bird opened an eye, it glowed orange. Herta stared straight into it. Without taking its eye off her, the bird stood up on the pillow, maybe twenty centimeters tall. The feather smoldered, the eyes burned, the creature squawked, and smoke rolled from its beak.

"Adolf," Herta named it.

The creature seemed satisfied with the new situation it found itself in. The fires died down, the smoldering stopped. It climbed up Herta's arm and perched on her shoulder.

"Is it hot?" Ernst asked, drawing closer.

The bird squawked and blew a smoke ring at him, and Ernst backed off.

"It is imprinted," Hagirr said, happily. "It will never burn you, Lady Hoffmann, even when it is engorged in flame. The same cannot be said for those around you if it is displeased."

Herta was smitten with the creature, a thing that was plain to see. A guard handed Herta a piece of meat that would have made a meal for Ernst, and she held it up to the creature. It took an engorging bite, the meat sizzled as the bird choked it down. Surprisingly, it ate the entire piece, which was half the bird's size.

"I have another gate to show you," Hagirr told Ernst. "This one will show you something I want."

This man, so powerful and overwhelming, had unmet wants?

"This way," Elianna told them as she started further down the hall.

The next frame they stopped at was different than the first. Similar in size, but instead of a rock face, behind it there was a mirror-like sheet of copper. Hagirr chanted and drew on the copper with various colored inks.

Ernst looked at Herta, then they both looked at Elianna for an explanation.

"There is a fledgling wizard on Aerth, a refugee from Earth. He's in the hands of a witch, Hagirr would like to save him and educate him properly."

Ernst nodded. A professional want, that he could understand. Hagirr likely had no material wants.

As they waited, the creature on Herta's shoulder purred not unlike a cat. Occasionally it would look evilly at one of the elves who grew too close, and a flame would smolder within the creature's eyes. It didn't react the same toward Ernst, although it did watch him cautiously. Maybe it smelled Ernst on Herta's skin and recognized him as her mate. Whatever was going on in the tiny brain of the raptor, Herta would have the best guard Ernst could imagine once the bird was grown. At the rate it was able to eat meat, that might be soon.

"Stand back," Hagirr warned, done with his drawing that was both complex and unintelligible. "We will look first."

The copper shimmered and the drawings vanished. Clouds raced past the frame, images of snow and foul weather. Coldness seeped into the hallway, making everyone shiver. The raptor snuggled closer to Herta and she smiled. Maybe it was giving her warmth?

The image swept groundward, and Ernst spied a camp on a narrow road by a small strip of trees. A cliff rose above the camp, and a steep slope fell away from the other side of the road. A small fire burned in a circle of logs. Two guards stood watch.

With rifles?

The frame settled on the road, and the men, the humans with rifles, raced to rouse their peers. They all wore primitive armor, but one of them appeared with a helmet that Ernst recognized.

These were British soldiers. And a tattooed monstrosity of a woman who drove fear into the heart with her very appearance. The witch Elianna spoke of.

Hagirr chanted and danced with his fingers, and suddenly it was clear that the British could now see into the hallway. Cold gusts blew in from the frame. The raptor squawked in displeasure.

"*Was sehen wir? Woher kamen diese Soldaten*?" Herta asked.

"You're seeing humans who have escaped into the wilds of Aerth," Elianna replied. "They overwhelmed their guides and fled, undoubtedly out of fear. We will try to deal with them gently, but the most important thing is we recover the Templar."

Hagirr was speaking to the others. The Brits raised their rifles, aiming into the frame. Ernst held his breath and pushed Herta behind him. The wizard and the witch exchanged insults, and Hagirr made threats. Then he wiped his hand across the frame, smearing the invisible writings and ruining the magic. The frame closed, returning to a now dirty sheet of copper.

The wizard looked enraged. He stood there for a moment, his hand resting on the copper, stained with the colors of the inks.

After a minute or so, he regained his composure. Ernst understood completely. He'd raged similarly before, and the true measure of a man was gaining control and pressing on.

Hagirr did just that.

"I have one more thing to show you in the pyramid," he told them. "I have a gift for you that will make the raptor and the amulets look like a pittance for beggars."

They followed him down the hall the way they came, but when they came to the original hall, they turned right, deeper into the pyramid. At the end of the main hall, they arrived at a large room with a very high ceiling. On one end of the room was a dais with a crystal on it. The crystal looked to be quartz, flawless, and cut into a hexagonal shape. It was amazing.

"When I tell you to stand in the black circles on the floor, you will stand in the two that appear where you're standing now," Hagirr told Ernst and Herta. "How old are the both of you?"

"I was born in 1897, I am forty-three," Ernst answered.

"Thirty-seven," Herta replied.

"Do your bones ache after all the walking we've done today?" Hagirr asked them. "Or every day?"

Ernst was getting very curious. Was Hagirr about to cure their aches and pains? "Some. And on most days. But that is life."

Hagirr laughed. "I am over twelve thousand years old."

"So Elianna said. It seems a ridiculous brag," Ernst told the wizard, then immediately wondered if it would be taken as an insult when Herta looked at him crossly.

"But a true one." Hagirr laughed, seeming to take no offense at all. "And you, my two newest friends, will benefit as I have." He turned to Herta. "There is a small cage over there on the wall I had brought for your raptor. Put Adolf in it, please."

Once she'd done so and returned to her spot, he turned and cast a spell into the quartz. Lights began pulsing on the other side of the glass wall. From below the edge of the window in front of him, so Ernst couldn't see what was going on. The pulses went on for a few minutes, then Hagirr cast another spell.

Black circles appeared on the floor. Long crystalline rods dropped down from holes that opened in the ceiling. Everyone in the room stepped into the circle nearest them.

Hagirr cast more spells, and the pulses in the other room quickened. Flashes of light appeared in irregular patterns, and suddenly Ernst's world was filled with light. He couldn't see, and a pleasure filled him like nothing he'd ever experienced before. He was afraid he'd drop to his knees, but an invisible hand held him in place.

Then, a minute after it began, the process was over. He looked over at Herta to see if she was okay.

Then he did drop to his knees, as the invisible hand had released him.

She looked sixteen again. Or at least how he assumed she looked then. She looked at him in astonishment. "Ernst, you're a baby!"

He felt his face. It was true. The blemishes of age were gone. He stood up from his knees without so much as an ache. They gasped in joy as they realized what just happened.

"We're young!" Ernst exclaimed as he lifted Herta from the floor.

"I will do this for you every twenty years, as long as our friendship holds," Hagirr said. He looked unchanged by the process, although he too had bathed in the light.

"Friendship holds?" Herta asked as Ernst put her down.

"I have helped you, now I have a small task for you in return," the wizard replied. "One critical to our worlds, and for the continuation of the magic that allows this," he waved his hand back and forth toward Ernst then Herta, "to happen."

A task. There was always a task.

Chapter 27 - Outer Barrier

It's hard to tell exactly when day and night happen underground. Luckily dwarves have the innate ability to know how much time has passed. None of Irsu's soldiers had even seen the sun of Aerth since they returned, but they knew they'd rested forty-eight hours in the underground oasis they'd found.

The sickly dwarves either hadn't followed them or went the wrong way up a side branch of the river. Either way, the dwarves had two days of rest and recovery. Clothes were dry, armor polished, bones warmed and bellies full. The only thing missing was a good tavern, but beggars can't be choosers.

Two rafts were loaded on the shore, packed with goods and places for the dwarves to sit and stay dry. Ropes, woven from mushwood fibers, were prepared and waiting for the pack lizards to haul the rafts further downstream. They had wood for camping fires, they even had a bit more food because Ekesstu had been generous. This river was indeed fertile, as was the oasis they were about to leave.

He and his squad were packing up their final items when to their surprise they were joined at the oasis. How, exactly, Irsu didn't know. He never saw them arrive.

Deep gnomes.

Irsu had met the deep gnomes several times, either as part of traveling trade caravans or mercenary guards on the caravans of others. The gnomes were renowned for their magical prowess and for their mechanical ability. What they lacked in strength and stature they often made up in guile and wits.

"Those rafts contain the property of Her Royal Highness, Ignesha of Arassticannik." The apparent leader of the gnomes spoke Undertrade, the language often used by different races to conduct business outside of their own territory.

Irsu wasn't wearing his armor, and his axe was a good ten seconds away leaning on a rock. He glanced at it, wondering if he'd be to it before the shortbows of the deepgnomes filled him with arrows.

"No need for that, at least not yet," the leader said, seeming to understand Irsu's unspoken question. "My name is Istarabbusnar, I am a Patroller."

He said that as if it should bear some significance to Irsu.

"I am a Patroller," Istarabbusnar said again.

"I am Irsu Cragstone, of Iron Mountain Hold," Irsu replied, choosing to ignore the last sentence the gnome said. "We are investigating an outbreak of sickness in a fellow dwarven clan. We know not what clan, or where they came from, but they attacked our hold, then disappeared into the deep ways."

"I see," Istarabbusnar said as if that was impacting his thought processes somehow. "And have you found anything out?"

"Not yet, we were attacked by a superior force on the bridge that crosses this ravine a few days up river."

"I know of the place," the gnome said. "It is a natural choke point on your underways."

"My underways," Irsu commented. "How do you get around if not by something like the deep roads?"

"Arassticannik is self-sufficient," Istarabbusnar said. "We do not need to leave our territory. We have everything we need as long as poachers are kept from ransacking our lands."

"We didn't know we were on your lands," Irsu replied. "You have no territorial markers."

"Did you think a spot like this just happened naturally?"

"I did," Irsu responded. "I've seen such spots before."

The gnome looked contemplative, and then a little less judgmental. "Maybe you have. I've never been out of my homeland."

"I can see that it bothers you we are here, on this amazing oasis. We will leave and be on our way," Irsu told him. "No need to overstay our welcome."

The gnomes laughed, which revealed the location of a few Irsu hadn't previously seen. They had the numbers. It would be best to resolve this without conflict if possible. He hoped the soldiers traveling with him were a lot more ready for combat than he was, just in case.

"You take from our land and plan to walk away without payment?" Istarabbusnar asked. The gnomes behind their leader readied themselves to fight, some rested hands on small weapons in sheaths, some tightened their grip on their bows.

"We didn't take anything made by your hands," Irsu replied, curious and a bit alarmed. "Just rabbits, a few trees, and some fish."

"The fish do not matter," was the reply. "The river is not our territory. The oasis, however, is the property of our queen, so there must be an accounting for the trees and meat animals you took."

Coragg whispered in Irsu's ear. "We have lots of fish, the river is laden. We can get more downstream. Perhaps a trade?"

"You say the river is not your territory?" Irsu asked.

"Correct, We aren't asking you to pay for the fish for that reason."

"We offer the fish to you as payment. We have a full dwarf-weight, dried and soaked in their own fat."

The gnome scratched at his goatee. "I'd have to see it, but if it's within the realm of the reasonable, I'll allow the trade."

"Coragg, take the fish off the rafts. We'll be a little lighter in the water, which is not a bad thing."

Coragg bellowed, and soon four dwarves sat two mushwood crates of fish on the sand near Irsu.

"Fish," Irsu offered. "In return for your queen's hospitality. Also word to our clan that trade with the Deep Gnomes of Arassticannik are fair and honorable traders."

Istarabbusnar inspected the crates, then turned toward his soldiers. "I, Istarabbusnar, patroller of Arassticannik, decree these dwarves of Iron Mountain Hold to be free of debt to her majesty, Ignesha."

The gnomes cheered, and instantly the tension fell away. The little people grabbed bundles of dried fish out of the crates until empty crates were left.

"I thank you, Istarabbusnar, for coming to an understanding."

Irsu looked at the back wall of the oasis. "How did you get here without us knowing?"

The gnome laughed. "I can't tell you how many would like to know that answer. Both enemy and friend."

Irsu nodded. He understood military and state secrets.

"I hope to see you again, Irsu of Iron Mountain Hold. You are a fair trader, and did not bring insult to us."

That was all they wanted, Irsu noted. Respect for their territory and their queen. Fair enough. "I hope we do, Istarabbusnar. Such a fair trader is a worthy find."

"Help them off," the gnomish Patroller ordered his soldiers.

A few scant minutes later the pack lizards were pulling the rafts into the center of the river. The gnomes watched from shore.

"Istarabbusnar, what is a Patroller?" Irsu yelled back to the gnomes over the sound of water.

"You would call me an Exactor, if I know anything about the dwarven equivalent," the gnome shouted back.

An judge and executor of justice.

"Well," Coragg said to Irsu. "At least he was a fair Exactor. Otherwise we'd be leaving here in our birthday suits."

"Or worse," Irsu corrected.

Chapter 28 - The Frailty of Men

July 23, 1940

They planned to walk along the shore once they returned to the north coast. Fortunately, Nelson and Gunter were both good navigators. They walked straight on toward Binic, just south of Étables-sur-Mer. They'd resupplied at the supply depot, knowing that whatever they took had to get them the nearly five hundred miles to Calais.

Nelson and his few survivors saw deaders six times in three days. As they neared the town of Binic they threw up a hasty camp in a copse of trees that would help them hide their cooking fire.

As they dug the pit for the fire, Billy walked into the area and grabbed Nelson's arm. He pointed toward the east, tugging at Nelson to follow him.

"Sure, Billy. Show me what it is."

He walked to the edge of the trees, and Billy pointed east once more. In the distance a different camp stood, with white tents and banners. A fire danced in the center of the camp, and Nelson saw men gathered around it.

Why weren't these men hiding from the deaders?

Something in his stomach told him to be careful, that people not hiding from the enemy probably were the enemy.

He nodded at Billy and gestured back toward their hidden camp.

"We have a problem," he said as he approached Gunter. "Another camp about a mile east."

"Good," Gunter replied. "We need more soldiers."

"I don't think it's our side," Nelson replied. "They ain't hiding like we are."

"Oh."

Nelson knelt over the small pit fire and warmed his hands for a minute. The night was cooler than he'd hoped for since they couldn't create much warmth.

He stood up, having decided a plan for the moment. He was tired of reacting, it was time to get some information. "Corporal Wilcox, you're with me. Bring your field glasses, we'll do some spyin'."

Wilcox grabbed his field glasses and his M1 Garand. At least the round from that rifle had a good punch. Nelson grabbed his own rifle, and they headed into the fields between them and their target.

"Why would anyone make themselves visible like that?" Wilcox asked.

"They ain't afraid," Nelson whispered back. "Either they are the cause of the deaders, or they have protection that works."

They worked their way to a few hundred yards from the camp. By this time, even without the field glasses, Nelson could see the men in the camp weren't men at all. They were the same skinny SOBs that he saw the day the enemy smashed the wall. Sure enough, they had horses hobbled on the other side of their camp. If they were there the day the wall fell, that indicated they were enemies in Nelson's mind.

Even if they didn't take part in the slaughter of Americans, they didn't stop it.

"What do we do?" Wilcox asked in a whisper.

"We watch, then we go back to report what we see. Then we figure out how we give these fellas a wide berth when we depart this place."

They scanned the camp for some time. The males of the skinny people were wearing armor that looked more like art than anything functional. There was a female among them, she was discussing something with the others, the center of their attention. For a brief moment Nelson considered sinking a bullet into her skull, but she stood up and looked in his direction.

It felt like she was reading his soul, but there was no way she could see him.

"She sees us," Nelson said.

"Nah," Wilcox replied. "She's just thinking, looking into the darkness."

"I don't think that's it…"

She stared toward them for nearly a minute before she tossed something on the fire. The campfire turned from an ordinary flame into a whirling column of purple inferno twenty feet high. Purple light illuminated Wilcox's face even at this distance.

"Get lower if you can, boy," Nelson told him.

They both did their best to merge with the ground, on a temporary basis, trying to avoid a more permanent association.

A figure appeared in the purple column. A figure like the

ones at the camp, but made of fire and eighteen feet tall.

"I am Trisari," it said, and Nelson understood the words perfectly. "The elimination of the threat is complete?" The words even had a Kentucky twang to them.

He couldn't hear the responses. But the character from within the fire sounded like he was speaking in Nelson's ear.

"There will be survivors, I'm certain," Trisari said. "Hagirr wishes them taken alive if at all possible. I will add to this Hagirr's orders. None of you are to risk your lives in the process of gathering in the stragglers. Let the dead do your work. You sweep up the remnants once they're all in a pile."

A pause as the female spoke.

Then the Trisari character again, "I don't know why these few remnants matter, but Hagirr says they do. Hagirr gives us what we want, in return we give him what he wants."

Pause.

"Because I said so. You're a sorceress of the court. If you can't complete your orders as given, let me know. I will banish you myself."

The female's gesturing increased dramatically.

"I will inform Hagirr of your loyalty. Do as you are bade. Do not fail. Your family is counting on your success."

The figure faded and the fire dropped suddenly back to the ring of rocks that contained it, returning to a normal orange and yellow.

"We've seen enough," Nelson said. "Let's go."

They made their way back to their camp, in the dark, moving slowly. The overcast skies would prevent them from being easily seen by mortals, assuming the skinny creatures saw like humans. But Nelson had no idea how the dead saw the world, or even if sight was involved. Maybe the dead smelled them out. On top of that, he wasn't nearly as sure as Wilcox that they hadn't already been seen. Something could be stalking them right now.

"They're not human," he told the three men waiting for them in camp when they arrived. "We heard part of their plan, and strangely, understood the words. Demonic magic, I'm sure. They have a mission to bring us and any other stragglers in alive. They control the deaders, and aim to use them to get us."

"They control the dead?" McKinney said. "Does that mean they're in league with Satan?"

"Ask your preacher when you see him," Nelson said. "All I know for sure is that Wilcox and I stared into the face of evil, and it spoke from the fire." He described that scene to them.

"God speaks from fire," Connors said. "Maybe we should do as the fire said."

"Son, I'll shoot you myself," Nelson spat out. "You need to quit talking crazy or don't plan on staying with us anymore."

He looked at the other three men. "We need to get some rest. One on watch."

They lay down and when Nelson opened his eyes again it was early light.

McKinney was laying on the ground, splayed out. Nelson roused him and McKinney groaned as he sat up. “Something hit me.” He reached for the back of his head.

“Connors is gone,” Gunter said.

Chapter 29 - The Temptation of Men

Two days after their encounter with Hagirr, Harry woke to Cylethe next to him. While he'd been faithful to his wife, Cylethe was making it more and more clear that she didn't want him to be. And the last few days she'd been attached at his hip.

It was time to ask why, it felt like something more was going on than her physical attraction to him.

They were off together getting water from a stream that wasn't completely frozen. The water steamed in the air, and Cylethe explained that the heat came from underground. The dek often watered their animals and drank from this stream during their journey to and from the winter grounds.

Now was as good of a time as any to ask. "Why are you with me every moment since the incident with Hagirr?"

"Have I been?" she replied.

"You know you have. You've also been uncharacteristically quiet."

She sank down to a squatting position, looking into the water of the creek. Without looking up, she answered his question. "Protecting Miller, trying to keep him from Hagirr… it might well be what gets me killed."

"By Hagirr?"

"Who else?"

He nodded. Indeed. Who else could destroy Cylethe? From

what he'd seen of her, his entire squad wasn't enough. With rifles. And not including the *drakon*.

Regardless, while he was fairly certain she wanted more from him, they remained friends. He would do what he could for her. "How can I help? You have taken us in your care, now let me do the same."

"We need to go someplace I'm loathe to go, where Hagirr can't track Miller's… enthusiasm for magic."

He laughed. "We'll go where you want. I've just been pretending to be in charge."

She flipped snow at him. "Don't be crazy. Your men would follow you into death. You're in charge, Harry. I'm even listening to you these days. You don't know how rare that is. But there is a reason that sword likes you."

"Because it hasn't seen a human in ten thousand years." He sat on a rock at the edge of the stream, free of snow by the heat of the water. The water steamed in the air. "Tell me what we need to do. I don't want Hagirr to find us, and I will do what it takes to keep you safe."

She batted tattooed eyelids at him. "Awww, you care Harry?"

"Cylethe, behave."

She shrugged. "We need to go underground. The Aldikki mountains are filled with underground dwarven holds, both living and dead. There are the underways, the dwarves built them for trade so they wouldn't have to come to the surface if they didn't want to. There are gnomes, orcs, goblins, gnolls and flinds, and elves down there."

"Underground? Are you sure about that?" It sounded silly, like a fantasy a boy might have playing with his friends.

"Harry, there are oceans down there. Rivers, and caverns so large they have mountain chains of their own. The deeper you go, the more diverse the terrain. There are free cities and kingdoms. It is an amazing place, although I've seen very little of it with my own eyes."

"How do you know it's real?"

"Grandmother told me."

That was good enough for Harry. It was real, although maybe exaggerated a bit. "How do we get there?"

"There is an abandoned dwarven hold a day from here, off the path, up through a pass above us. We can get there. The hold was conquered and sacked thousands of years ago, but it is an avenue to the below that we can get to quickly."

"Then why do you seem worried?"

"It will be filled with creatures, some harmless, some dark and terrifying. My drakon will not be with us."

"I always found you more terrifying than your *drakon*," Harry told her, grinning.

"You've seen nothing. I never ask him to deal with something if I can do it alone."

"Fair enough. I assume that's your policy for everyone."

"Not for you, Harry," she said. "Like it or not, you're my choice for *konsikt gai*. Or *konfrelt gai* if I can convince you."

Konsikt gai would make him her pre-marriage playtoy. "*Konfrelt*?" he asked.

"Promised."

"Oh, no. I'm married," Harry replied. "I told you—"

"The heart wants what it wants, Harry." She looked sideways at him, uncharacteristically shy. "You will see. And I wouldn't feel this way if there wasn't something in you that felt the same. We dek are emotionally sensitive creatures."

"Nonsense," Harry replied, a bit addled in his thoughts. "I am married."

"A world away."

He didn't say anything. She was smarter than him and knew more about how things worked in this world for certain. She always talked circles around him.

"You think about it," she told him, standing up. "A wizard is always more powerful with the emotions of a relationship to drive them. The stronger the bond, the stronger the wizard becomes. It's why Hagirr and Elianna have each other, and it's helped him grow very strong to have the love of an elf." She grinned wickedly. "You loving me might save the world."

"Why haven't you found someone before now?"

"Fate. None were worthy. You're a leader. A human mate will make me stronger. Plus, I respect you. I will follow you."

"You don't seem the sort to follow anyone."

"As I said, none were worthy. And by follow you, I actually mean I will listen to what you have to say before I do what I want."

He decided to change the topic; he felt his body responding in ways he didn't like. He was certain his face was flushed, and he was involuntarily reacting to her in other more obvious ways that he hoped she didn't notice.

When he'd met her, she'd scared him with her differences and her strange ways. Now there was something different when he looked at her, he had to admit. He didn't see tattoos; he saw a trusted friend. He didn't see the filed teeth; he saw a smile. He didn't see a terrifying witch; he saw comfort and faith.

It was infuriating and confusing.

"Let's get the men ready, we move toward this dwarven hold. Can we be there before darkness?"

"Yes, we can. The trip there will be the easy part, although still very hard. The hold itself will be potentially dangerous, as I said." She rested her hand on his shoulder. "Miller and I could go there alone, and you and your men can follow this trail to the winter grounds."

"A repugnant thought, that I'd abandon you. And that you think I would."

She grinned her pointy-toothed grin and touched his face. "You do care."

He shook his head. Now that she'd made her choices toward him, she was going to be very persistent. As if his life wasn't hard enough. "Of course I care. About you and my men. Let's get going."

"Fine. You will break. Males always break when they're meant to be a female's *konfrelt gai.* I am fertile, if you're wondering. And yes, I know the humans and dek are a sterile pairing. But I can use magic to give us a child, if that's what you want, but you'll be doing most of the raising. I've never been with anyone else because I can't risk pregnancy. The last thing I need is to have a child to lead around by myself."

"Cylethe, the topic is finished. I'm married."

"Of course you are, Harry." She started walking back toward camp, brushing up against his leg. "But to whom?"

He growled his frustration. She knew full well what she was doing. She was, when he met her, ugly as a goat. When he'd met her she smelled like one too. Now she was starting to smell like happiness. Her personality, her confidence, it was overwhelming. It was the most absurd thing that had ever happened to him.

And, to make it even worse, *Dynamus* liked her.

"You know she's not human, right?" he whispered to the sword.

Smugness. Damned sword.

Chapter 30 - The Sacrifice of Men

July 23, 1940

He was young again! Ernst never felt so good in his life. At least not in his memory. That feeling alone made the challenge of whatever task Hagirr might have seem almost welcome.

The vigor of youth flowed within him like a freight train.

Herta was just as amazing, her body was tight, her skin flushed with vitality, and her passions expressed with wanton abandon rather than concern for a muscle strain.

Hagirr had given him three days to just enjoy the sensation. The sex was amazing, the gluttony, the exercise… it was all beyond belief. He hadn't appreciated it the first time around. Now he savored every moment.

When the three days were up, Hagirr and Elianna took Ernst and his wife back to the Pyramid of Souls, and once again into the room where he and Herta had been reborn.

"I thought I'd bring you back here so you'd understand the monumental value of what is at stake should you decide not to work with me on the task I have for you."

The *task* again. It had to be dealt with. "What task?" he asked the wizard directly.

"It's more of a reward than a task, really. I want you and your lovely bride to rule Germany, and eventually Earth. If I understand the political situation there as described by Elianna, then that situation should serve both worlds well."

Ernst realized that his jaw had dropped. Hagirr looked

amused.

"You want me to rule Germany." He shrugged. "How do I accomplish this — task? What should I do, just march into the *Reichstag* and announce that I am the Führer now?"

"You'd have Elianna at your side. And potentially a legion of my elvish troops if you need them. But I don't think you will. Elianna has her own resources."

It was hard to keep his sarcasm in check. "And they'd just say 'sure, Ernst, it's your turn now' and I'd be Führer, just like that."

"Ernst!" Herta said, scolding her husband. "Show some appreciation for the generosity of our hosts!"

"I do," Ernst said. "But one does not simply walk into the *Reichstag*, or the *Reichskanzlei*, and take over."

"It's fine," Hagirr said, waving to Herta in a gesture that suggested she should remain calm. "Ernst and I are cut from the same cloth. He isn't a fool who rushes in."

"No, he's not," Herta agreed.

"Ernst, I will be with you," Elianna said, taking Ernst's arm in hers. "Do you think that Hagirr would put me in danger?"

"Of course I don't think that," Ernst said, aware that the body chemistry of youth had removed most of his fear of Elianna from his thoughts. He should choose his words carefully. "But he doesn't love me as he does you."

"Not yet," Hagirr laughed. "You're growing on me, however." The wizard motioned toward the exit. "I'd like to show you how this magic you've benefited from works."

"Ooo, I'd like to see that," Herta said.

"You need to be of stout constitution," Elianna warned. "It's not pretty. I know Ernst can handle it, Herta, but you've not seen what he's seen."

"I can deal with whatever it is," Herta replied, indignant.

Hagirr took Herta's arm and dragged her along. Elianna took Ernst's, and the elf gave him a look that it was best Herta didn't see. Hagirr led them down the hall toward the flight platform, then took a side path. This one wasn't as decorated as the others, and what carvings were in the walls were much darker in nature.

Demons tearing at the bodies of humans and creatures. Monsters consuming the flesh of large numbers of people kept in confinement. Murder of all sorts. Torture on the order of Dante's Inferno.

"We go down here," Hagirr said, as a stone wall slid back and then to the side. A stairway circled downward, and a musty smell greeted them. The air whistled past them up from the descending staircase, seemingly eager to escape the depths of the pyramid.

They descended a good twenty stories. His new young body didn't seem to care, and neither did Herta's.

They reached another tunnel that moved into the pyramid in the direction of the room they'd regained their youth in. The hall was arched, the center was several meters high. The floor was at least four meters wide. Guttering sconces adorned the walls, no magical lighting illuminated their way. The smell of burning oil greeted their nostrils.

"Straight ahead," Elianna said.

They walked a distance that Ernst guessed would put them directly under the revitalizing room. A golden door was, by far, the finest object in the hall. It stood on the left side. Closed.

"This is our destination," Hagirr told them. "Open the door, Ernst."

Ernst looked at the wizard uncertainly, but what option was there? If he refused his host, he estimated his life would be measured in seconds. He pushed open the door, noticing that Hagirr seemed to enjoy his discomfort.

A stone room with a window on the top wall, a good fifty meters up or more. A stone pillar stood in the center of the room, floor to ceiling. Piles of dust lay around the room, on the floor. Articles of clothing lay in the dust.

"That is the Focus," Hagirr told him, pointing at the column. "It is what gathers the energy that has made you young." Hagirr walked into the room and a single patch of arcane writing lit up on the pillar. "Come in."

As Ernst entered the room, another patch lit up. When Herta and Elianna followed one more patch lit up.

"It recognized us when we walked in the room, but not Elianna I'm guessing?" Ernst said. "It functions using humans… and humans only, somehow?"

"Very astute," Hagirr replied, acting impressed. "You're right about him, Elianna."

Ernst walked to a pile of dust and picked up an article of clothing. A jacket. “This is a French uniform. This dust is what remains of a Frenchman you brought here?”

“Again, on the mark. At least I assume so. I don’t know what a Frenchman is. But you’re one hundred percent correct about the dust.”

“Elianna?”

“Yes, Ernst. This machine turns the souls of humans into life force for whoever stands in that room above,” she said, pointing up at the window. “That is the room where you were both rejuvenated. Thanks to the rabbit-like proclivities of the humans of Earth, there doesn’t appear to be a shortage of souls.”

This was the most monstrous thing Ernst had ever seen. He knew of the campaign against the Jews in Germany, but that was an unseen thing, out of his domain, and senseless since it wasted valuable manpower. This was the slaughter of the innocent to benefit others directly. Ernst himself had benefitted. What were his feelings on that? Normally he tried to ignore the complications of morality, but there was no choice now. He had to decide quickly where he stood on the matter.

Hagirr walked up to Ernst, face to face. The wizard put his hand on Ernst’s shoulder and looked him in the eye. “Ernst, my friend. You will rule Germany as you see fit. Your people, or whatever fraction of them you deem worthy of protection, will prosper. Those you deem unworthy you will send through the gate to Aerth.”

“Just like that?” Ernst said. “I will round up the fodder for your machine?”

Shrugging, Hagirr smirked. "If not you, then someone else will do it."

"I bet that von Krosigk fellow wouldn't blink an eye," Elianna tossed into the conversation.

"Ernst, these were Frenchmen, not Germans. They were sacrificed for a greater good," Herta said. Ernst thought she might be enjoying her tight young body a bit too much to be unbiased, but he understood that sentiment. He was enjoying his too.

"This is a horrible thing you're asking me to do," Ernst told Hagirr. "If I do this thing, this task, when I die my soul would be black as night and doomed to torment."

"That's the beauty of it." Hagirr walked away from Ernst and kicked one of the dust piles on the floor. "There are so many of us humans on your world, you will effectively be immortal. You will have your heaven in this life."

"Ernst, please," Herta begged.

She was smart enough to figure out their situation, Ernst was sure. Either he agreed and their moments became without number, or he said no, and these would be their last moments.

"I agree," Ernst said, quietly.

"Good," Hagirr said, jubilant. "We must get you in power as soon as," he laughed, "humanly possible. Then we find this Ark of the Covenant Elianna speaks of and we destroy it."

"As you planned to use me for all along," Ernst said to Elianna, more than slightly accusational in his tone.

She rolled her eyes. "Don't make this dramatic, Ernst. You're a king among humans now."

He felt more like a monster. But if there was to be a King of Earth, who better than him? He would decide who was fit to live in the greater glory of the human race, and who would die.

Then a thought of solace hit him. The Italians, he mused, would have to be marched through the gate. Insufferable people. He hated them. That Duke in Ethiopia would be among the first.

"I see you embracing it," Hagirr said. "Come. A feast for the rest of this day, and a celebration across the city before you return to claim your throne."

Führer Ernst Haufmann. It had a good ring to it.

Chapter 31 - Enemies are Legion

The dwarves were drawing near to the end of their first day of travel past the gnomish alcove. They'd fashioned hooks from wire, and cord from an old pair of pants that were packed on the lizards by the dwarves of Iron Mountain hold for some reason. The eclectic collection of goods on the pack lizards made Irsu wonder if they hadn't just thrown everything onto the beast in a haste to reach their carrying capacity. That diverse selection would give Irsu's squad every opportunity to use what they could.

Then he considered the circumstances of their departure. Of course that's what they'd done. And they'd been right to do so. A pair of worn out pants that seemed useless were now catching fish.

Which wouldn't be necessary if not for the gnomes.

"Are they following us, you think?" Irsu asked Coragg.

"I would," Coragg said. "We're not enemies, but we're clearly not friends either. Stay on the river, or we camp on the trade road on the right side would be my advice."

"They did say they didn't claim the river, so the other side should be fine."

The dwarves had made good time with their new rafts. Irsu had no way of knowing how far they'd traveled, but the pack lizards were moving faster pulling the weight instead of carrying it.

That night they camped as Coragg suggested, on the hard-worked stone of the trade road, which someone carved to a certain point then stopped. Probably to trade with the very gnomes that had taken their first fish stocks. A small sand bar jutted from the edge, providing a place for a fire and where they could cook. Whoever built this section of road might consider it vandalism to burn a fire on it, so Irsu was grateful for the sand.

The soldiers continue to fish, catching fat blind catfish to sear in their pans. If there was any sort of underground predator nearby, the smell of the fish would draw them. Irsu ordered one third on guard, two thirds asleep at any point during the night. He and Coragg would take middle watch with two others, as that was the most unpleasant watch.

His first sign of trouble was from the pack lizards. They began to dance uncomfortably on the flat of the road, ready to flee. They were hobbled, so that wasn't going to happen, but Irsu knew to trust their senses.

"Wake the men," he ordered Coragg.

Three minutes later fourteen dwarves stood in an arc around the lizards, crossbows at the ready, shields facing outward, axes within reach. Halstim, a younger member of the troop, spotted the enemy first.

"Eyes," he hissed.

Sure enough, malevolent greenish eyes appeared out of the darkness on the road downriver, the remaining light from the dwarves' campfire being just enough to reflect off retinas and alert them to the creatures.

Several sets of eyes bobbed up and down in the darkness.

"Shield wall," Coragg ordered, and the dwarves reassembled within thirty seconds. Now the line of shields faced the eyes, with a taper toward the river to protect from a flank attack. Stone wall guarded their right.

One set of eyes drew closer. A snow-white dire wolf with a rider.

The rider stepped down and walked forward. Whatever it was, it was brave. It stepped enough into the light to let Irsu see what he needed to see.

An orc. An important one considering it wore metal armor and carried a metal weapon. Most orcs were barely more than animals who made do with what they had at hand. They followed their leaders because of fear, as far as Irsu knew.

"*Singo pastinik sha-ambi*," the creature said.

Irsu had no way to understand it. There was no reason to bring a translation amulet on this trip. He'd planned to pick one up in Iron Mountain Hold before he left to conduct his investigation.

The orc didn't seem upset that nobody answered him. Instead he stared at the dwarven line for a moment, then walked to the edge of the river and started gathering pebbles. Satisfied with his collection, he returned to the center of the trade road and looked at the dwarves once again, this time with crossed arms.

"It's like he's saying he'll wait," Coragg observed.

Irsu pulled his shield away from the wall. "Close ranks behind me. Be prepared to let me back in."

"Bad idea," Coragg said, but stepped aside to give Irsu more room.

"I'm full of them."

Irsu stepped toward the orc, who grinned as he approached. Large canines told Irsu that this was a meat eater, and one with less than perfect care for his teeth. One canine, on the bottom, was larger than the others. It had a hole bored through it. A gold chain dangled from the tooth; the bottom end had the desiccated head of a rat on it.

"I'll call you Mouse," Irsu said.

"*Imtushi na'ak sungonor*," Mouse replied. The orc knelt down and placed pebbles in a line on the ground. Fourteen pebbles. He pointed at the dwarven shield wall.

"Okay, that's us," Irsu nodded.

"*Imtushi na'at sungonor*," Mouse said, almost repeating what he'd said before. He took one of the stones and held it in his hands. The rest he pointed at, then pointed downriver. The last rock, in his hand, he popped in his mouth and chewed on.

Fourteen traveled. Thirteen may travel on. Irsu got it. The toll for passage was one of them. As food.

Irsu held up a finger and walked back toward his line. Coragg opened a hole for him to rejoin.

"Shield wall strong, stand low, prepare for arrows," Irsu shouted. "Advance on my order in two beats. We will kill these soulless dogs."

"Mordain!" the dwarves shouted as one.

Irsu looked over at Coragg, who was grinning.

"We have no idea how many of them there are," his second said. "What did he say that made you so quick to fight?"

"The toll to pass is one of us. As dinner," Irsu replied.

The grin disappeared quickly. "Mordain!" Coragg shouted.

"Mordain!" the soldiers responded.

"Advance, one TWO!" Irsu shouted. The shield wall advanced two steps. "We will advance until we're out to the zone of light the fire creates. When our night vision returns, we attack," Irsu told Coragg. "Unless they press matters earlier."

"Advance, one TWO!" he shouted again.

The shield wall inched forward in a process that seemed all too slow.

A heavy weight slammed into the wall, growling and spitting on the dwarves behind it. Coragg shoved his axe over the top of the wall, piercing a wolf in the throat. The beast fell, whining like any dog would. Numo, who was not part of the shield wall, put a blade through the creature's eye, into the brain.

"They're testing us," Irsu shouted. "Advance, one TWO!"

"Mordain!"

"I wish we had pikes," Coragg griped.

"If we survive this, we make some," Irsu agreed. "Advance, one TWO!"

Arrows were next. The pack lizards were unprotected, taller than the shield wall, but they had thick hides that might protect them to some degree. The number of pings against the shield wall was telling to how many orcs they faced.

"Twenty, maybe twenty-four," Coragg said. "Unless they're holding back."

A pack lizard roared in frustration behind them. One of the arrows must have found it. Hobbled, it couldn't do anything but protest.

As Irsu glanced back, Numo was moving to tend to the arrow.

"Numo, let the beast be," Irsu ordered. "You're to kill anything that breaks this line."

"Aye," the scout replied. "If it panics, it could hurt the other beast as well."

"Advance, one TWO!" Irsu yelled. Numo had his orders.

Arrows struck them three times. One soldier took a shaft to the calf, just above his boot. No armor was perfect.

"Ready bows," Irsu yelled, grabbing his from the loop over his shoulder. Coragg took a bolt and placed it in Irsu's bow. The movement was repeated down the line, allowing loading with one hand as the other hands held shields. Now every other dwarf was armed with a shot.

"Advance, one TWO!" he yelled. After waiting for the warriors to reply Mordain, he continued. "Hand off the shields!"

This was a dangerous maneuver, if the enemy charged, the line wouldn't be able to withstand it as one dwarf held two shields.

"Bows over the top!"

The shield bearers stooped and lowered the wall. The

crossbow wielders took aim down the hall at the green eyes. Now that Irsu could see them, he realized they were backing away. Apparently, they'd not seen a dwarven line before.

"FIRE!" he yelled.

Seven bolts fired downrange. It was customary to pick the target most directly in front of the shooter, so Irsu estimated that six, maybe even seven targets were hit. The crossbows were powerful enough that only dwarven armor would stop the bolts. Howls from beasts, the yelps of pain, the swearing of the riders let Irsu know the bolts had found their marks.

"*Andimar*!" someone yelled from the darkness ahead.

"Bows down, full shields," Irsu yelled as he set his down and took his shield from Coragg. "Axes ready to bite!"

"Mordain!" the soldiers yelled.

"*Andimar*," sounded again from the other side, then a few seconds later a horde slammed into them.

Swords and sticks plunged through any hole they found in the wall, nicking a few of Irsu's soldiers. Nobody said a word that wasn't needed. The grunts, cries, and sighs of battle were only broken by an occasional growl. The enemy stabbed where they could, Irsu's soldiers responded with axes, turned around so the pointed haft could be used as a spear, and thrust back through toward the enemy.

"Blood!" a soldier would yell. If the target fell as the dwarves advanced, Numo dragged the orc through and slit its throat. Blood covered the stone as Orcish lives pumped out onto it. The road would soon be slick with blood at this rate.

Irsu needed to continue the advance, to keep the enemy unable to build a strong defensive wall and provide secure footing for his soldiers.

"Advance, one TWO!"

"Mordain!"

"AGAIN! Advance, one TWO!"

The orcs weren't able to stand up to the sheer strength of the dwarven soldiers. They were being pushed back.

Suddenly one leapt on top of his peers, then vaulted over the wall. The creature was immediately engaged by Numo, who took a dirty stab to the shoulder from what looked like a wooden knife. Right before he disemboweled the creature with his short sword.

"Numo is hit," Irsu said to Coragg. "They'll try that again. Over and over until they bleed us out."

"Half-circle, wall at our backs," Coragg suggested.

"That will leave the pack lizards open."

"I favor us, not lizards."

Coragg was right. "Half-circle on the wall," Irsu yelled.

The dwarves cautiously, but quickly. changed their line to a semi-circle facing outward from the wall on the right side of the road. That would foil the leaping tactic for the moment, but it meant that the orcs now had access past their position on the road.

"Two archers tighten the line," Irsu commanded.

Two soldiers, the best archers Irsu had, moved to the center of the arc, reloading and firing as fast as they could.

Orcish hands grabbed the top of Irsu's shield, he was unable to find a mark for his axe haft on the other side. A head pushed over the top, and just as Irsu thought the creature might pull him down, a bolt from one of the arches split the beast's face open. The foul thing fell back into the mass of his brothers, pulled away so another could take his place.

"This is more than twenty," Irsu said.

"I was never good at math," Coragg shot back. "I'll apologize after we win this."

A dwarf two down the other side of Coragg fell, a spear shaft through his throat. One of the archers sat down his bow, dragged his fallen comrade back, and filled the hole.

"You're an optimist," Irsu said, as he thrust his weapon into an orc. "Maybe you should apologize now so I actually get to hear it."

"Pfft. We've been in worse. At least these aren't living dead."

Irsu grinned. It was true.

"We're not done here," Irsu growled, as he flipped his axe around, preparing to give the order to break the wall.

Just that moment a flash that seemed brighter than a hundred suns lit the cavern. Orcs shrieked, and the smell of burning flesh reached Irsu's nose. While anything that distracted or harmed the orcs was a good thing, the smell of cooking orc wasn't pleasant.

The remaining orcs broke and ran screaming, Irsu's soldiers waited for orders and blinked their light-blinded eyes. Normally he'd order them to take down the fleeing orcs with bows, but nobody could see well enough to shoot. He could barely make out the faces around him.

At least three dozen spinning balls of blue-hot luminescence raced down the road, so bright that Irsu couldn't help but involuntarily look. When the spheres hit an orc or a wolf, the creature died, dissolved from the inside out by the blue energy. Each went down to the stone of the road screaming until their lungs disintegrated. Even as their heads rolled away from now missing shoulders the pain was evident on orcish faces. Until the head dissolved as well.

"Half-circle wall!" Irsu ordered. The dwarves solidified their position, but Irsu knew that whatever had decimated the orcs, they were no match.

Istarabbusnar appeared around the other side of the wounded pack lizard, carrying a still glowing staff.

"Justice is dispensed," the gnome said.

Chapter 32 - Pursuit

July 27, 1940

They were being followed. Nelson had no doubts. New dead fell in behind them, creating greater and greater numbers to remind Nelson's team that south was a way no longer open.

They'd grabbed a truck, because it was obvious now the deaders knew where they were. Travel was quicker, they covered ground fast, the roads were empty. Despite the noisier mode of travel, and despite the fact the enemy obviously was aware of them, the dead didn't get too close. There was an unspoken agreement.

Do what we want, and we'll not bother to kill your squad. For now.

New deaders always filed in behind them, replacing the ones the truck left behind.

"There is no escape," the deaders told him with their actions.

Their herders wanted them to go north. He'd been moving his crew north, and toward the coast of the English Channel, with a plan in mind.

Probably suicidal plan.

"Honfleur," he told Gunter. "There is a small bay there, if we can make it to the boats, we can try to cross the channel."

"You remember that British destroyer, right?" Gunter said, his voice skeptical.

"D-48? I do."

Unconvinced eyes stared back at Nelson.

"How common do you think those monsters are in the channel?" Gunter asked.

"Does it matter? Right now I reckon we're being herded to captivity of some sort. Or a large feast where we're the main course. If we get a boat at least we have a chance."

Gunter thought a bit in silence as they rode along.

"You're right," he finally agreed. "I just wanted to make sure you knew the choices were a chance at being food or almost certain captivity."

"I ain't surrendering," Nelson replied. "Whatever they're herdin' us north for, it ain't for our benefit."

They drove on through the French countryside, discussing their plan, taking turns driving as the other three rode in the back.

The maps Nelson had didn't share much detail about the harbor, but it would almost certainly have smaller boats of some kind. And it was just the five of them now with Connors' insane betrayal and likely death. They wouldn't need more than a sailboat.

A motorboat would be better. With a full tank. It was, judging by his half-worthless map, a hundred miles or so to the south of England.

Plenty of space for roaming sea monsters.

They made Honfleur early the next morning, with no indication from the enemy that they were concerned with the course the Americans were taking. It was still north, after all. Once the town was in sight, they made their way into it, heading straight to the harbor.

"Plenty of boats," Gunter said.

"We need to pick one, and fast," Nelson told the men. As he finished his sentence Billy grabbed his arm. Something Nelson was getting used to. Whatever was wrong with the kid's voice, it hadn't addled his brains.

The giant pointed toward a motorboat on the other side of the harbor, near some apartments overlooking the calm water.

"Can't you get one nearer, Billy?"

Nelson didn't know if the kid knew anything about boats. It looked like the one he liked was a shiny, rich-kid boat.

"That's a runabout," McKinney said. "Fast, should get that hundred miles past us in about two, two and a half hours."

"You puttin' me on?" Nelson asked.

"No, Sarge, I'm aware that the monsters are out there too. Billy's right. That's the one we want."

"Then we better get running before the enemy gets here."

They sprinted down to the point of the harbor, and around to the south side. By the time they started west again along the apartment fronts, deaders were spilling past the corners of buildings and moving toward them.

"They're onto us," Gunter said.

Nelson didn't have much breath to waste. "You think?"

They made it to the boat, the dead horde maybe fifty yards behind them.

"Push off," Nelson yelled. "Anyone know how to run this thing?"

The men didn't answer but threw the mooring lines away and pushed off from the dock. The boat floated away from shore all too slowly.

Billy sat down in the driver's seat, but there weren't any keys.

"Move over," McKinney said as he dove under the dash. He ripped wires down and started cutting at them with a pocketknife.

The dead piled up against the water's edge, then pressure from behind pushed some off. Those unfortunate enough to be in the front plunged into the water. It looked like the water was about eight feet deep. Despite a deep green color, Nelson could see the tops of heads as the dead slowly walked on the bottom.

"Hurry, McKinney," he ordered. "Everyone shoots except you, McKinney. Billy, you be ready to drive."

Gunter, Wilcox, and Nelson shot bullets into the heads they could see. Still, it was only a few minutes before hands were scrabbling against the side of the boat trying to find purchase and climb in.

The engine sparked.

"More of that," Gunter barked. "Now."

The engine turned over and growled to a start with a deep rumble.

"Sit down!" Billy roared.

Everyone did, in the seats that wrapped around the back part of the boat in front of the engine. As the last butt hit the Fabrikoid seats, the boat shot forward like a banshee.

"Billy, you spoke!" McKinney said.

The big kid didn't answer. It would appear he only spoke when it really counted.

Billy hammered the boat into the channel, as McKinney moved to sit by the usually mute driver.

"Fuel?" Nelson asked.

"I don't know," McKinney said. "Looks like a thirty-gallon tank maybe... but at least it's full. We need more than three miles per gallon to make it."

"Is that something we can pull off?" Nelson pressed.

"It'll be close."

Billy made a sign like he was zipping his lip, and the others grew quiet. Nelson had no idea why he was taking orders from a mostly mute giant, but the kid seemed to know what he was doing. Now and then he'd look up at the sun to get a view of where it was and adjust his course slightly. It was early afternoon; the channel was far calmer than Nelson thought it would be. At least considering the wind back on land.

They were, at last, away from the deaders.

For now. He didn't honestly know what shape Britain was in.

Half an hour later, a creature broke the surface a few hundred yards east of them. A massive snake-like beast, completely different than the one that took out the destroyer and submarine. It flailed out of the water and raced toward the runabout.

It stayed the same distance behind them. Unable to gain, for now.

"I think I peed myself," McKinney announced.

"Keep your problems to yourself," Gunter told the private, a sentiment to which Wilcox agreed.

The creature didn't give up, however. It breeched the surface behind them, again and again, roaring its displeasure.

"The tank is at two thirds or so," McKinney told them, looking inside.

Everyone looked at Billy.

The young man smiled. Good enough for Nelson, and it wasn't like Nelson could make a difference anyway. Nobody here was pissing out any high-octane fuel.

By the time they spotted the British coast, the creature behind them had vanished. Either by distance or underwater, which was a thought Nelson didn't like at all. Would it move faster underwater?

As he questioned the possibilities, he heard a familiar sound. Aircraft.

Two Spitfires raced overhead, from south to north, the same direction the runabout was moving. Three of the Americans, including Nelson, waved wildly at the planes. There was no way they weren't seen; the Brits were no more than two hundred feet off the water. He knew for sure the fighters had seen them when they passed over again, waggling their wings.

Fifteen minutes later more planes appeared, from the opposite direction, from England. Four Spitfires, and four ungainly monsters. Flying boats, maybe?

As the aircraft neared the runabout, the new arrivals began flying in expanding circles, as if searching for something.

A few minutes after that a trashcan like object dropped from one of the flying boats and splashed into the sea behind Nelson's squad.

A tremendous uproar of water followed, turning the sea white. Water burst fifty feet into the sky.

They were bombing the creature. Nelson was right. It moved faster underwater. If the planes were accurate, it was no more than a quarter mile behind.

McKinney looked into the tank. "Wow."

"How much?" Gunter asked.

"Maybe a gallon."

They were still miles from shore. It wasn't enough.

The planes concentrated on the area of the sighting. The sea serpent leapt from the water at a plane overhead. As it did so a different Spitfire strafed it. The RAF had learned how to bait the beasts.

Another geyser of seawater shot toward the sky. If these bombs didn't kill the monster, then it would get his team. They had to slow down to save fuel if they wanted to reach the coast. So far, their nemesis showed little concern for being shot or being bombed.

"Sarge," McKinney said, patting his shoulder.

He was pointing west.

A boat was racing toward them, a roostertail of spray behind it. Some sort of military shore patrol, it looked like.

A flare fell from the sky over the last area the flying boats had bombed, and the second boat raced past them toward that spot.

Brave souls.

As it passed under the red smoking flare that was still floating down toward the water, the patrol boat rolled barrels off the back end. Each barrel was released about two hundred feet apart, Nelson estimated.

The sea erupted. He wasn't sure the Royal Navy hadn't blown a hole in the channel floor.

The boat, now empty of barrels, swung toward the Americans, pulling up alongside at what Nelson estimated must be over thirty knots.

"Hello, mates! Can you stop for a moment? We mean to take you on board." The sailor threw a rope over to the runabout so the two boats would stop together.

"I've never been more grateful for anything in my life," Nelson yelled back.

Three minutes later the patrol boat was back underway, and the now abandoned runabout sat bobbing on the water behind them. Nelson watched it from the deck, grateful for the little boat even though it would now be lost.

Almost as if to prove his point, the water near the runabout broke and the serpent rolled out and over the small craft. Splintered wood flew through the air, then it was dragged under.

A British officer standing next to him clapped his shoulder. "Lucky lads, spotted just in time."

"You guys bombed that thing into next week, sir," Nelson said. "I can't imagine how it's still alive."

"Oh," the sailor replied. "We've only ever killed one. Most of the time we just manage to stun them and buy some time."

"How do you know you killed one?"

"Well, the head, you see, it's sitting on the Parliament Square, next to Robert Peel. A spectacle to let the British people know it can be done. We have a dragon head sitting near Nelson's Column in Trafalgar Square."

"They can be killed?" Nelson asked.

"Yes, sergeant. It can be done."

He looked at his men, his fellow Americans, who stood from their seats and walked up to Nelson and the British officer.

"Then we're here to help," Billy said, extending his hand to the Brit.

Dammit, Nelson was going to say that.

Chapter 33 - Down Under

Harry didn't really like what he was seeing. A giant gate, ripped from its hinges and leaning against a stone frame. The door was two feet thick, and despite the age of the structure, the wood, whatever it was, looked like it was cut yesterday. Wind whistled out of the darkness; a warmth gusted across Harry's face. It smelled of stone, dampness, and… well… death.

Two large dwarven warrior statues, carved from the stone of the mountain, stood eternal watch next to the gate. Not that they'd done a good job.

Cylethe sent her drakon away, to the winter grounds. Grandmother would take care of him, she told Harry.

He was sad to see the beast go. It felt like they were being disarmed.

"Whit removes a door lik' that fae tis hinges?" Lars asked.

"Your guess is as good as mine," Cylethe said, urging the team and the horses forward.

"'An' yi'll waant tae gang in thare then?" he exclaimed, throwing his arms up in the air, then looking incredulously at Harry.

"Remember the chap in the magic window, Lars?" Harry asked. "He makes anything we find in there look like a kitten. That fellow wants to abduct Miller and kill the rest of us. This is our one opportunity at survival."

Miller walked next to Harry as they passed under the base of the torn off door. "Lars is right. This is something I must do, but not you. Not them, Lieutenant. Hagirr isn't after you."

Dynamus let Harry know it didn't believe a word of that. Hagirr was a dire threat to every person in existence. Particularly humanity.

Miller shook his head and then tended to one of the horses, helping guide it along the rubble on the floor of the massive tunnel they were walking into. The young man was feeling guilty, but there wasn't anything for that. Other than to show him that this particular squad of the 5th Infantry Division, 25th Infantry Brigade, 4th Battalion didn't leave men to fend on their own.

"Private Miller, last I checked, I was your Lieutenant. You are a private, you work for me. I would be more likely to fold the underwear of the Queen of Denmark than let you face this terrible place alone."

"Alright, we have twelve of us, counting our esteemed friend," Harry said, gesturing toward Cylethe. "We will have six of us with crossbows in hand at any one time, ready to shoot. The other six will be tending the duties of the horses, or the issues of our expedition such as food or water. Any chat from this point on will be whispered unless we know our surroundings are secure. I'm certain you all will do what is proper to keep the rest of us and yourselves safe."

"Release the horses," Harry ordered. "Carry what we need the most. Hopefully the faithful beasts will survive, but they can't go where we're going."

A few minutes later the horses were fleeing toward the open air as the squad's goods lay about in chaos.

Harry stuffed the most important things in his pack. Food,

warmth, ammo, and a way to carry water. "Pick it up, we need to move."

Cylethe, clearly annoyed with the delay, walked past him. "Let's go."

They descended nearly two miles, by Harry's reckoning, straight into the mountain. Sloping halls, stairwells, and at one point a creaky wooden and iron elevator. Once below, and at the edge of the hold, they came to another gate much like the first. But this one was still on its hinges. Towers rose floor to ceiling on each side, with murder holes looking down over Harry's men. The good news was that they were all quiet.

The gate was closed, but someone, or something, had chiseled a small passage under it. A man had to crawl through, like being born again, to the other side.

"This is why you sent your *drakon* to Grandmother?" Harry asked.

"It is. I've sheltered in this hall before, but never gone farther." She gestured toward the hole under the door. "Goblins. To some of them that is a roomy passage. To others, not so much."

"They get fat?" Miller asked.

"Sometimes. Or just big."

"I'll go first," Miller said.

"Step off," Harry demanded. "We will rotate who goes first in such situations, by rank. From the top. I go first."

"No." Cylethe looked angry and shook her head.

"You said you would follow. Do so."

Harry slipped off his pack. His hands held only his rifle as he passed through, although *Dynamus* was still on his back. He'd tied a rope to the pack to drag it through after him. He sensed fear from the sword, but whether that was for Harry or because it didn't want to be lost in some hole in the ground for another ten thousand years, Harry couldn't say.

He stood up on the other side in a darkness that dripped into his eyes and down into his very being. A staleness filled the air, and in the distance something clinked. Water dripping on metal? A creature? In blackness this complete, he had no way of knowing.

Cylethe came next, she immediately took up position behind Harry.

"*Sangilanti nal Ingustik*," she whispered.

A bluish white light appeared about fifty yards ahead, and maybe five yards off the floor. Bright, it illuminated everything between them and the light, plus another fifty yards beyond.

Machinery filled the hall floor, the walls of which were worked stone. Pillars rose along the sides, and doors led off into chambers unknown. The machinery was mainly siege weapons of such apparent age that some of the iron was beginning to break. Sections of machines had fallen to the floor.

After what seemed like an eternity the squad was once again standing together.

"Is Miller safe here?" Garrett asked.

Cylethe shook her head. "No. This region will be where

Hagirr looks hardest. Miller's presence will fade to him as we go deeper underground, and he will know why. He will send hunters after us, and they will know to come underground. Spectral hounds will track us long after our scent is gone to regular dogs."

"Cheery," Jenkins added.

Harry didn't need squad morale to drop. He was going to talk to Cylethe about openly sharing the truth. She needed to filter it through him first. "Then if safety lay deeper, let's get going."

He didn't want to know what a spectral hound was, although he probably should. He'd ask later, in camp.

They moved deeper into the dwarven hold, the main hall past the gates was immense. They were surrounded by pillars keeping a ceiling that invisible above in place, and that disappeared into the darkness on each side.

"We could get lost here," Burke whispered.

"I suppose we could," Miller replied. "But the center path is clearly marked. So our light would have to go out for that to happen."

"You know what I mean. This place is bigger than anything I've been in before. I bet this one chamber is larger than Buckingham Palace."

"Yes. It probably is. We'll be fine, we have Cylethe."

Miller seemed to be growing in confidence now that they were in the hold. Maybe the thought of possibly surviving this ordeal was seeping into his brain.

They walked along, probably half a mile, over carved flooring that had just enough relief to give footing to their boots. The dwarves considered everything in their building. Eventually they came to a large conical structure with stairs up. The stairs aligned perfectly with the path they'd come down.

"The public throne," Cylethe whispered. "Usually trapped in some fashion. We should go around, look for the back doors out of this place."

"Semchikook show you!" a voice called from above. "Semchikook know back door!"

Six crossbowmen immediately stood ready, and the rest of his men scrambled to do the same.

"Semchikook not dangerous, just hungry," the voice called out again. "But not for you." A figure appeared at the edge of their light, up on the public throne stairs. It walked toward them.

A creature with yellowish skin, long lanky limbs, and a bulbous belly under a dirty white robe stopped ten yards away. With a face not even a mother could love, the thing stood no more than four feet high. "Semchikook not fight. Semchikook goblin of peace."

"Or a thief," Cylethe said.

Harry was amazed he could understand it.

"No, you mistaken dek. Semchikook priest of Semesku. Aspect of fire."

"And still maybe a thief," she repeated. "Prove you're a priest."

“*Detoobisnar,*” Semchikook said, and fire appeared above his outstretched palm. He sat it on the floor, and it crackled merrily like a campfire. A campfire with no wood.

“Semchikook wish to travel with dek female.” The goblin stepped closer. “And with creatures he not see before.”

“Well, you are a priest,” Cylethe said. “And still maybe a thief. Let me talk to my friend.”

Cylethe took Harry to the back of the squad while the men pointed their bows at Semchikook in case he got any ideas.

“He seems harmless enough,” Harry said. *Dynamus* sent a wave of approving emotion into Harry’s awareness. “*Dynamus* likes him. This sword knows things.”

A different sense of warmth flooded into Harry. The sword liked to be appreciated.

“That is a good sign, but we’ll have to watch him if we let him come along. Goblins are notoriously deceptive.”

“Fair enough. But that fire ability seems useful enough. Especially in a place like this where fuel might be scarce.”

“I’ll need to determine his rank and power within his faith. A strong Semesku priest is a force to be reckoned with. But he summoned a fire, not an elemental, so I’m guessing he’s pretty much an acolyte.”

“Or discreet,” Harry replied. “He’s not you.”

She grinned. “Maybe.”

“We let him guide us then?” he asked.

"We can, but we keep a good eye on him until he proves himself. We'll also need to know if he can heal."

"You mean bandage? Use a poultice?" Harry asked.

"No. Magical healing. It's very rare, and a sign that a deity favors that priest greatly. If that's the case, then it will increase my estimation of him."

Harry turned back toward the goblin. "Semchikook, do you have access to magical healing?"

"Oh yes, creature I do not recognize. I do."

Cylethe cut her finger with a knife and walked forward. "Prove it. If you're lying, you die here."

"*Scoonibo dal poosti,*" the little guy chanted, reaching out to touch Cylethe's outstretched hand. The wound closed immediately, as if it never existed. "No die today," the goblin said, giggling.

"We bring him," Cylethe said, turning around. Her eyes widened as she seemed to realize she was trying to take charge. "With your approval, Harry, of course. But I recommend it now."

"Then it's done," Harry agreed. He looked at Semchikook. "You take the lead. We will follow. Do not betray us, it will not go well."

"Semchikook earn your trust! Semchikook good."

Soon they were standing by a gate much like the one they'd entered the dwarven hold through, but considerably smaller.

"*Togrug nog sempitook,*" Semchikook said to Harry. "*Scal nogro dwarvi noost.*"

"What?"

"His spell that allowed you to understand him has expired. He says we need to open this gate to get to the underways."

"Great, another language barrier." Harry sighed. It didn't matter. Semchikook was too valuable to let go if his intentions were honorable. "Then let's get it open and be on our way."

Shortly after, with the gate open, they took their first steps into the uncertain pathways that lay ahead. Miller might be safe for the moment, but they had to keep moving. And they had to stick together. If they could find more allies, like the goblin priest appeared to be, then they'd stand a chance.

"You worried, Harry?" Cylethe asked.

He looked at his men, at Cylethe, at the goblin staring at him with bulbous eyes.

"We live, or we die. At this point, living is the outcome that matters."

Lars coughed. "Ah wale bide, ye best dae th' identical, lieutenant."

Harry laughed. "That is the plan we're going with Lars. We all want to live." He turned toward the underway to steel his courage.

They all looked into the inky blackness ahead of them, pausing a moment to push down the natural fear that men have of such places. A new phase was beginning, and instead of leaving this world Harry was delving deeper into it. Time would tell if his choice saved lives, helped anyone, or ever got his men home again. But he would try. And that effort started with the next footstep deeper into the darkness.

"Let's begin," he said to the men.

Cylethe walked beside him, and without a word, the men filed in behind.

Chapter 34 – Insolent

Elianna glared at the servant girl entering the room with her wine. The idiot was taking too long to do her assigned task.

"Tell me, child, are you aware what happens when I or Hagirr find disappointment with a servant?"

The servant lowered her eyes, but not before Elianna recognized fear. "I am, lady. I am sorry, someone failed to refill the decanter on this floor."

"Oh, really? This wasn't your fault?"

"I should have noticed and reminded them, lady."

Elianna stood and walked to face the child. She towered a full head over the servant girl. "I asked you a question. Was this your fault? Did you fail in your task through your own actions?"

"No, m'lady."

Turning to the guards that stood in the doorway, Elianna smiled. Sweetly she said, "Bring me the palace vintner. You have five minutes."

The guards raced out of the room. They were there for show only, only one person in the palace was any real threat to her. And, fortunately, he loved her.

He walked into the room as she thought about his love.

"What's this?" he asked.

"What's your name, child?" Elianna asked.

"Niza, lady."

She looked at her beloved. "Niza had to go to a different floor to get wine. We do have a vintner who is supposed to prevent such a delay, do we not?"

"We do," he replied. "Just kill her if you must kill someone, the vintner has useful skills."

"Those skills aren't keeping the decanters full."

He waved his hands in surrender. "Do as you wish; I have no doubt you will anyway." He looked at Niza. "It's your lucky day. Leave us."

"No, she stays. She needs to see this."

The guards raced back into the room as Hagirr started to reply, then tossed an older dwarf onto the floor. He stood up and dusted off his vest, looking at Elianna and Hagirr. He bowed deeply. "Lord. Lady."

"Vintner," Elianna began. "What is your job here?"

"To ensure the palace has wine, lady."

"Then why is my decanter on this floor empty?"

"I wasn't aware it was, lady. I filled it two hours ago."

"*Ingustin de mogussne vir*," Elianna chanted, as a look of fear filled the dwarf's eyes.

He dropped to his knees, crying out in pain as his skin blackened and the entirety of his eyes turned blood red.

"You will suffer agony for three days. If there is a time during those three days I don't have wine at my beck and call, anywhere in the palace, you will die. If you survive the three days, I will release you."

Hagirr laughed even as the dwarf struggled to raise himself from the carpet. "You're like a cat."

Elianna smiled and ignored him otherwise. "I suggest you find a way to make sure you do not fail. Your death will be spectacular." She gestured toward the door. "Crawl away."

The dwarf did as told. He crawled out the door, stoically trying not to cry out. The result sounded like a restrained grunt.

"Go tell others what you have seen," Elianna ordered Niza.

The girl fled. Her fear indicated she was very aware that the dwarf's suffering could easily have been hers.

Hagirr shrugged, then spoke to Elianna, still facing the door the young girl had departed through. "You will be returning to Earth. Shall I release the dwarf in three days or do you intend to kill him anyway?"

Leaving so soon wasn't Elianna's plan. "Dearest, I will return to Earth in a week with your approval. Ernst and Herta need more time to learn the delights of power and youth."

"I grow tired of your projects. We should simply crush this Germany and sweep their people into the gate."

"My plan is better," she said, "but if you feel that strongly about it."

He sighed. "No, I have enough to worry about, you're dealing with this. A week then." His sigh turned into a grin. "The longer you are in my bed anyway."

"Germany is near to the gate. They will be our funnel for the human race."

He stared at her a moment, looking serious. She wondered if he was reconsidering, but then he broke out into a relaxed smile. "They think this will work out for them as the rulers of Earth," Hagirr said, laughing once again. "That part of it entertains me, so I grow more enthusiastic for your plan. Imagine when we turn on them."

"Ernst and Herta are not to be harmed," Elianna warned.

Her tone seemed to shock her lover. "You dare to order me?"

She walked up to him, pushed her splayed fingers into his chest hair. "Indulge me."

Shaking his head, he pulled away and sat in a chair, taking Elianna's wine that Niza had brought.

"I always indulge you. You are pampered. Maybe it is time for discipline?"

It was her turn to laugh. "You could take me down, but Jangik would be a smoking ruin before it was done. We both know this. You may be the most powerful wizard on Aerth, but I would be shocked if I'm not second."

"Maybe," Hagirr agreed. "I do not wish to see my jewels destroyed. You or Jangik. Let's not test our skills today."

"What are your pets doing with their time?" he asked.

"Making love, eating, engaging in play. Much like we do."

He grimaced. "Do not compare anyone to us." Taking a drink of her wine, he swished it about his mouth, almost as if he were washing the taste out. "One week. Then you take them to Earth and install them as puppets."

"Easily done. All the more reason not to hurry them."

"I understand your reasons," he said. "But Earth must be emptied of humans. It will take years, and I wish to get started."

"You will have your souls. You will have your slaves. You will have your beautiful human women."

"I know. I always get what I want."

"Since you gave me a week, I would think that so do I," she teased, sitting in his lap and stealing back her wine.

"Insolent."

She clasped his face and kissed his lips. She lay her cheek against his and whispered into his ear.

"I know. I always get what I want."

<<<< To Be Continued >>>>

Authors Notes:

First, I'd like to apologize for taking a long time to get this book out. I could make excuses, but they don't mean a thing to you, the reader. You want books. It's my job to provide them.

I will endeavor to improve on that.

I do have another book in my Dark Seas series coming out soon if you like science fiction. Just look up my name on Amazon and you'll see the details on my author page.

As you can see from the story, this world has almost completely diverged from ours in just a few months. I've killed off Hitler and stopped the war in Europe cold in its tracks. It is still on in Asia, for now, and you can see that in Chapter 1. Expect the war to expand in the coming novels.

I am hoping that with the trend on social media to eliminate anything that might offend someone, factual or not, that we don't lose our ability to research WWII and the atrocities committed during the war. YouTube is deleting any references to the Nazis, even educational videos that stand against fascism.

When we cannot refresh our minds, we forget. I hope that something changes, and the media giants realize just how important our history is. It's even more important not to scrub it into a generic tale in order not to offend anyone.

Please remember the losses our ancestors suffered. On the fields of battle, in the concentration camps, and in the green fields of China. WWII was a very dark time in our history.

Never forget.

Printed in Great
Britain
by Amazon

31368512R00151